Stroud clapped on his hat and took a squint at the sky. It was still overcast though the storm in the south seemed to be blowing itself out. With his glance coming down again Stroud's shape went rigid.

This hogback which formed the pocket's east rim fell sharply away beyond the ragweed and nettles in a kind of gulch or ravine and what had caught at Stroud's interest was a section of roof with a stovepipe sticking out of it.

Off to the left of him he heard brush break and he turned half around to his right and started running, not toward the fence but parallel with it and away from the pocket. A gun went off somewhere back of him and another gun barked somewhat closer and to the left, and he caught the high whine of ricocheting lead. Scared, but more angered, he stuck to open ground where the sound of his travel would not so quickly betray him. He heard a garble of voices and an enraged shout tearing through them: "There he goes, damn him—cut him down! Cut him down!"

All hell broke loose then with at least three rifles trying to knock the legs from under him. . . .

NELSON NYE
THIEF RIVER

C

CHARTER BOOKS, NEW YORK

THIEF RIVER

A Charter Book / published by arrangement with
the author

PRINTING HISTORY
Previously published by Ace Books
Second printing / September 1981
Charter edition / May 1987

ISBN: 0-441-80611-2

Charter Books are published by The Berkley Publishing Group,
200 Madison Avenue, New York, New York 10016.

PRINTED IN THE UNITED STATES OF AMERICA

MAN AND WOMAN

"WELL, no, ma'am, I sure don't—I'm new around here myself," Stroud said, blowing some of the drizzle off the end of his nose. He leaned forward, scrinching up his eyes in the rainswept dark, trying to make out the faces of the pair in the buggy. "There's some town up ahead mebbe three-four miles—could see the lights of it 'fore I come down off the bluff."

The man's head moved. "That'll be it," he sighed. "That'll be Thief River."

Stroud said, kneeing his horse in closer, "If there's any—"

"No. We'll make out," the old man assured him. "The Lord looks after His own . . . 'Yea, though I walk through the valley of the shadow, I will fear no evil.' That old boy knew what he was talking about. Thanks, young feller, but we'll get along . . ."

His voice trailed off through the drip of the rain. Stroud heard the skreak of the buggy seat and the old man's hand came out through the curtains. "Here— speakin' of comfort, try some of this."

Once again something clawed at the edge of Stroud's

thinking. But he was tired with too many hours in the saddle, chilled with the damp of this sodden night. He thought: *To hell with suspicion and caution,* and up-ended the bottle.

The teeth of that brew bit clean down to his boot-soles. With tears in his eyes he passed back the remainder. "Prime stuff," he acknowledged, still fighting for breath.

The old coot chuckled. "Lee's Elixir—good for man or beast. Good for kidney complaint, sour stomach, clogged bowels, sallow complexion or screw worms. Guaranteed to grow hair on a hitchin' post. . . . Well—" he said, lifting the lines and clucking—"take care of yourself," and the buggy rolled off, its sound quickly lost in the drone of the rain.

Long moments Stroud stayed where he was, looking after it, trying to dredge up something too vague for remembrance.

He sighed, shrugging it off with a twist of broad shoulders, settling deeper in his slicker and kneeing the roan into weary movement. Mike Stroud at twenty-three had more pressing things to do with his time than cogitate over patent medicine peddlers.

Lord, but he was tired. Tired of pounding leather, tired of this drizzle and tired, above everything, of recurrent thoughts. He'd decided this thing a couple thousand times and there was no damn sense thrashing through it again.

The slosh of the downpour slacked off a little. Beyond the black shapes of the sodden pines bullfrogs were croaking, remindful of a night he had sworn to forget.

The frogs had been caterwauling that night, too. He

had heard them riding up to the shack where Vingie's note had asked him to meet her. How clearly he recalled getting off the bay horse, the feel of the spongy earth underfoot, the eagerness with which he had opened the door. Every step of the way, each sound, smell and detail, remained crystal sharp behind the shutters of memory, complete to the point where he had opened that door. Beyond that point his mind refused to go.

IF that was Thief River he had glimpsed from the bluff, three nights of riding had brought him farther than he'd guessed; and perhaps it had, he decided, considering the condition of his horse.

Few men, these days, ever thought of Thief River though it had once been a common enough name on folks' tongues. *Too tough to die* men had called it in the arrogant vigor of its boisterous nights, but it was quite as dead now as Curly Bill Brocius. True, a handful of desert rats and possibly a dozen old crotchety cowmen still managed to scratch out a living in this locality but it was as forgotten by the most as Galeyville or Charleston. It belonged to the past and most folks figured to leave it there.

The edge of a twisted smile tugged Stroud's lips. Then he caught the wet glimmer of lights through the murk and the time for making up his mind was at hand. Unless he decided to stop a spell here he had gone far enough along this trail.

He was minded to flip a coin, but luck was a fickle goddess and one he had small faith in. A man made his own brand of luck, Stroud believed. It was the things within himself, he thought, which put a man's boots to one rut or another. Environment and circumstance were the excuses of weaklings, and he did not class himself in that category.

He scraped a damp hand across beard-stubbled cheeks. The rain-drenched gleam of those distant lights sang a siren song to the blood in his veins, reawakening hungers as old as Adam. There were certain fundamentals common to both hounds and hares and what a man carried with him was not altered by whereabouts. This was as likely a place as any—perhaps likelier. One thing was sure. As certainly as water finds its own level, turbulence in the genes of a man would find its outlet in violence.

These truths acknowledged, Stroud sat his horse on a rise above the river and rummaged the lights of the town with sharp eyes. The rain, he presently noticed, had quit and a rustler's moon was poking its face through a ragged rent in the clouds still brooding with sullen mutterings above the crags of obscured peaks.

Yonder, bluely spread with the splendor of distance, lay all the vast country of the Superstitions, land of lost trails and tumbledown shanties, land of black malpais and memories. There, too, lay Thief River and all that remained of an outlaws' rendezvous, reduced through the years to a handful of shacks that, like gray ghosts, stood scabrously creaking along the dark street. These, and a ramshackle pole corral, still stood as a monument to past greed and perfidy. The rest was gone, scoured away by the desert winds.

The great river itself was no more than a drinkless trickle, unable even with this rain to make aught but a futile gurgle. Its melody was gone with the gamblers, pimps and prostitutes, the hardrock men and the muckers, the merchants and bleach-eyed gun fighters who

4

had known this place during its glorious youth. Thief River was a bent old harridan now, ugly with bony hands and lewd smirks, mouthing her tale of bright yesterdays.

The lights Stroud had seen were in the three largest buildings. Crowding the tie rails before each of these was a clutter of buckboards and wagons, interspersed between which he saw the shapes of hitched horses. And it came over him with something of astonishment that this was a Saturday night, the one night of the week or perhaps the month during which Thief River roused to draw another breath.

It might be, after all, more practical to move on. News of a stranger would have flown fast enough had he entered this town on any other night. To come into it now was to invite attention.

He sat a moment considering this and then, with a shrug, sent his tired horse ahead.

He passed the cold smell of a blacksmith shop and turned into the weed-grown street of this place, the fogged shining of its lights through the rain streaked windows making of the puddles bright pools of blood against the quivering flesh of the hooftracked earth. Red earth this was, a kind of roan vermilion that went very well with what he knew of its past.

By its batwing doors he would have known the nearest building for a lamplit saloon. Talk and the clink of lifted glasses came clearly into the street's blurred shadows; and a rider moved out of the dripping trees and cantered toward the porch of a store, also lighted, arriving there just before Stroud himself did. It was a girl with a slicker rolled back of her cantle.

She rode astride in a skirt hiked up by the saddle,

disclosing bare legs which Stroud eyed with approval. She caught his look without blushing, left the skirt where it was and got out of the saddle on the big black's far side. Dangling her chin-strapped hat from the pommel she went into the store without looking back.

Stroud sat there a moment and then got out of his oilskin. With his eyes straying again toward that lamplit door he had his plain impulse and disregarded it.

He did not look just now like a man born to trouble though he looked like one who had seen his full share. Tough with the weathered endurance of granite, he was a middling tall man with a high flat shape and eyes the color of smoky sage.

A slow wind moved off the river, earthy and damp with the smell of wet pine. The swell of Stroud's shoulders rolled faintly and his glance ducked across to the yonder saloon while he listened to what this night had to tell him. Care and vigilance were ingrained parts of him though he sometimes chose to ignore their promptings—as now when he smiled and stepped onto the porch.

There were eight or ten people inside the store and their eyes wheeled to watch him as he moved to the counter where a hanging lamp thrust his gaunt face into shadow.

He tossed a coin to the clerk and asked for Bull Durham and stood there and waited while the clerk went to fetch it. He felt like a strange dog among that still group, unconsciously bristling as they covertly studied him.

The girl stood by the yard goods with two other women; the rest were all men in the garb of their calling. All conversation had fallen away with Stroud's entrance and none seemed called upon now to resume it.

Boots pulled sound from the floor behind him and a man's voice said: "Gaunted roan. Strange brand," and a serge-suited fellow next to Stroud coolly nodded while his glance stayed at work and the silence built up again, tighter and tighter.

Having expected all this Stroud kept hold of his temper. "Seems I got into the wrong road someplace. I been headin' for Globe—is there a trail cutting into that country from here?"

The clerk, cheeks inscrutable, came back with the Durham and laid down Stroud's change.

By the stove a man said: "Hell! Throw it back at 'im!"

Nobody else said anything.

"Globe," Stroud repeated—"don't any of you know how to get up to Globe?"

The clerk turned his head and spat into a corner. Then he rested his shoulders against the crammed shelves and gave Stroud back stare for stare without speaking.

Stroud looked at the other men standing around and saw himself being fenced in with suspicion. He picked up his money, aware that these things ever followed a pattern. In the minds of this crew any stranger who came here was either one of two things; and a remote kind of smiling laid hold of his lips.

"Well, thanks," he said and, wheeling round, started out.

"I'll show you the trail."

It was the girl with the corn-yellow hair and green

glance, the one whose bared legs had attracted Stroud's interest. Stroud's eyes locked with hers in a long, searching look.

"I'll show you the trail," she said, coming toward him.

2

THE PRIMROSE PATH

THE man in the blue serge suit flung a hand out.

"You lookin' for work?"

Stroud's stare took him in from boots to black Stetson.

He was young, young as Stroud, with a bigboned muscular look about him. Sun and drought had baked his cheeks and the highbridged nose, with those bright and caustic eyes above it, gave a bold and lively look to the face which was not belied by his bluff, assured manner.

"If you're lookin' for work—"

"You got any?" Stroud said.

"I might give you a job if it suited my book."

"And whose book is that?" Stroud came back at him, pausing.

Something made its brief shine in the big man's eyes and then they crossed the girl's face and he said with a chuckle, "Stirrup's my brand—I'm Dan Wafer," as though that settled it. "You can put your truck in my wagon and hole up at the saloon till I'm ready to leave."

"I can," Stroud said. "What kind of job?"

The black eyes danced back to him, bright and quick searching. "Don't worry about that. I'll fit you in."

He was turning away when Stroud said casually, "If I decide to hole up here I'll keep it in mind."

WAFER'S face came around, half surprised, amused even.

"Maybe you don't catch the picture. This town isn't partial to drifters. You work for me or you roll your cotton."

Stroud pulled Durham smoke into his lungs. He let the cigarette drop out of his hand, grinding it into the floor with his boot. He told Wafer then in the softest of voices: "I'll go when I'm ready."

The big man's mouth shaped a wintry smile. The girl came forward, pushing Stroud toward the door.

The night outside seemed cool, filled with freshness. In the light from the window Stroud saw the girl's face. A frank interest looked out of her eyes. "Careless and reckless. Or pretty sure of yourself."

The quality of her smile upset Stroud's coolness. He half swung toward her and then stopped without speaking.

She seemed almost to invite his inspection. She had no false modesty and returned his look with the frank directness of a man. There was a vibrant magnetism about her; like the nearness of lightning it was heady, disturbing.

She said abruptly: "Make no mistake about Wafer. He won't forget that business. You better not, either."

"I understand," he nodded, and her smile cut deeper.

The green eyes laughed. She lifted an arm and gestured north. "The trail you asked for cuts off through the hills just beyond those shacks."

She stood thoughtful, still studying him. "Are you bound to take it?"

The third lamplit building, which appeared to be chiefly some manner of hall, showed signs of life as the string ensemble of a sagebrush band commenced tuning up with a thwacking of fiddle strings. Off someplace in the coalblack shadows between that building and this porch where they stood a woman said quickly, "Not now, Joe—not here," and a man's grumbling voice rose and fell and was lost in the boisterous racket of three passing riders who swung down by the hitchrack in front of the hall.

Stroud said, sighing, "Don't you reckon I ought to?"

Her eyes were the color of new-mown alfalfa.

"Does it matter what I think?"

He looked down at her, wondering, more than ever disturbed by the directness of her gaze.

She said: "I don't think you much care what you ought or ought not do. If you were the cautious kind you would not have come here in the first place."

Stroud turned that over. He said whimsically, "Does a thing always have to be black or white? You're thinking I'm either a tinbadge or fugitive—"

"I wasn't much carin'."

He looked at her carefully. Though her head didn't come much above his chin she was tall for a girl. She wore a man's hickory shirt unbuttoned at the throat, its tails pressed flat against flexible thighs which embossed each fold through the cheap cotton cloth of her short figured skirt. Her legs were bare and quite shapely and the sleeves of her shirt were rolled to the elbows.

She might have been some pagan priestess incanting a spell as she stood there. Like a high wind the nuances of her personality swirled about him, caressing and confusing; an alchemist intent upon dethroning prior convictions. There was something strange and primeval about her, a challenge that called to the unthinking depths of him, an unusualness that excited his senses.

She was like no woman he had ever known. A fierce and yeasty pride worked in her, yet she had grace, a strength of assurance that endowed each gesture with an odd allure that was doubly provocative. She was, he supposed, in that first lush ripeness which presages maturity. Yet she knew what her appearance could do to a man—it was a knowledge openly flaunted in the laughter that crinkled her eyes.

He saw how deep breathing bulged and tugged the shirt's buttons. He watched her red mouth curve into a smile.

"You're a damn pretty girl," he said, gruffly.

"You didn't know about me when you rode into this place."

He had no answer for that so kept silent, listening into the sounds of this storm-troubled night, indefatigably translating them while his glance hungrily prowled the girl's face and some facet of his mind kept picking and probing at her reason for having come out here with him. All the hard facts of his life bred suspicion and even the siren song of her youth, tumultuous, bewitching and powerful as he had found it, could not entirely submerge a habit so much a part of him.

No girl such as this one would go out of her way to swap talk with a drifter without some good reason. She hadn't come out here just to point out a trail. She was up to something and he couldn't for the life of him decide what it was.

Not that he doubted her interest; it was the quality, rather, of that interest which bothered him. Why would she appear so taken with a stranger? Boredom? Monotony? Dissatisfaction with her lot? If he read the signs aright she was offering him that trade which girls in the backlands frequently held out to any personable stranger who would take the responsibility of getting them away.

Yet she did not look dissatisfied. There was no boredom in her face or talk. He had no reason for thinking she might want to quit this region. She didn't want to leave. She wanted him to stay here.

Mike Stroud was not a fool. He resented being taken for one—particularly by a woman. This girl hadn't actually offered him anything; she'd merely lifted the tent flap a little and trusted man's greed to take care of the rest.

He eyed her again and didn't like any part of it.

She didn't look nervous. Nor was she nearly so cool as she would like to have him think. Now she said, as though on impulse: "I'm Lucinda Lee—you can call me 'Cindy' if you like."

Stroud guessed he was supposed to consider that a favor; and maybe it was. He considered several angles and finally gave his own name, covertly watching her for any sign of recognition. But there was none, nor did she answer.

He commenced to shape a smoke but let the paper

flutter away when her hand pulled him into the shadows. Almost at once someone opened the door and Dan Wafer came out and went down the porch steps, pausing to throw a quick look toward the hall, then turning and striking off briskly in the direction of the horses hitched before the saloon.

Her hand tightened. She leaned across him and, sensing the acuteness of her interest, he looked after the man and saw another step out of the darkness and stop him just out of the light from the saloon's batwing doors.

The girl whispered: "Link Craftner!"

If it was this second man she meant it was all right with Stroud; but the girl squeezed his arm again and he remained silent, watching. Though in the shadows themselves the pair, from Stroud's angle of vision, were silhouetted against the saloon lights and he could see Craftner only as a tall, cadaverous shape whose features at seventy-five yards were indecipherable.

Wafer's words, though low held, crossed the interval plainly. "You fool!" he growled. "Haven't I—" And that was where the sagebrush band turned loose its mixed fiddles on the Irish Washwoman, and anything the pair said after that was as safe from Stroud's ears as though it had never been spoken.

The girl's hair brushed Stroud's cheek. "Let's get off this porch."

He followed her off across the puddled road. In the deeper gloom of the trees she stopped and faced him. "Do you have to get to Globe? Right away, I mean?"

Now she was coming out with it. She had a use for him, all right. He'd been correct about that part. Whatever she had in mind it plainly called for a stranger and the need, in her own mind at least, was urgent.

"Well . . . supposing I decided not to shove along just yet?"

"You might regret it," she admitted, "but if you're the kind of man I think you are—"

"What kind of man is that?"

"Look," she said quickly, putting a hand on his arm again. "They're having a dance here tonight. Would you stay long enough to take me?"

The fragrance of her hair set up its own intoxication. He knew folly when he saw it but, after all, was only human. He took her arm with leaping pulses and grinned goodbye to caution.

3

REHEARSAL FOR DEATH

HE knew an ironic satisfaction moving out of the trees
with Cindy's arm hooked in his. The night wind held a
keener flavor and the earthy smell of drenched vegeta-
tion kicked the blood through his veins at a fine loping
tempo—or was it this girl's nearness which made
things seem different?

He glanced at her covertly. Her green eyes were
fixed in a cold still attention on the black shapes of men
grouped about the open doorway and the foreshortened
view he had of her jaw gave plain and ample warning
there'd be trouble over this. He was backing her hand in
some kind of open rebellion and he no longer cared
about the reasons behind it.

A mood of recklessness was on him that could take
perverse delight in ignoring the probable aftermath of
indulging in such folly. Safety was for shop clerks and
other cud-chewing cattle—*life* was for caballeros who
had the guts to face it. A guy was either man or mouse
and Stroud thought it might amuse him to play David

with a slingshot and thumb his nose at this country's
Goliaths.

He gave Lucinda's arm a squeeze to get that scared
look off her cheeks; and then they were tramping into
the light and men round the door were twisting their
necks. He saw gusts of expression reshape startled
faces and then they were past, going into the hall, with
the stamp and din of *Sally Gooden* avalanching to
enfold them in the squeal of fiddles.

This place, Stroud saw, was mostly used as a
schoolhouse. One end was stacked with piled-high
desks but the black-boarded walls still showed chalked
problems and one had a picture some wag had labeled
Teacher. Among the old folks and children assiduously
warming benches, wallflowers lifted their toothy
smiles and sighed and simpered at every gent below
fifty.

Stroud was a little surprised to observe such a crowd
in what was practically a ghost town. "But they come
from all over for this kind of a doings," Cindy told him.
"The Bartletts over there came clean from Elgin."

Then her willowy back was moving away from him,
lithely skirting the hilarious antics as she made for one
of the less crowded benches, Stroud following. *"And
all promenade!"* the caller cried, and they were caught
in the rush of seat-hunting dancers. When the tide
receded all the benches were crammed and they stood
marooned in an island of others on the open floor.

It rather seemed as though they might become a
sensation.

All over the room there was a twisting and stirring
and most of this movement, Stroud realized at once,

had himself for its focus. Too general to be based on identity, it must obviously have sprung from his proximity to Cindy. Some of these folks stared in openmouthed astonishment; others reflected an interest which he sardonically thought remindful of a glimpse of the Roman masses just before the half-starved lion got its hooks in the squealing Christian.

He had little time to ponder. A man had come out of the group just beyond and braked to a stop three feet away.

The place had been noisy with many conversations but now a sepulchral quiet closed down and the slant of Cindy's cheeks presaged action.

She had her eyes on this new man and they weren't green now; they were the color of gunsmoke. "Hello, Ben," she said.

He was a snake-hipped man, gaunt and rawboned and gangling, his bony face framed in a chin-strapped hat. Freckles, like paint, blotched the skin at his cheekbones and his eyes were bright with an affronted anger.

"I want you to know Mike Stroud," Cindy smiled. "Mike—meet Ben Redcliff, our sheriff."

THE girl's casual words held all the shock of a bullet. They cocked every muscle in Stroud's scarred body, but nothing disturbed his wind-ruddied cheeks from their look of polite faintly wistful gravity. He held himself ready for whatever might happen and wondered what purpose this girl was now serving. Whatever her game it was obviously desperate.

Redcliff's arrogant eyes slanched one look at Stroud's face and went blackly back to the girl's cold regard.

"If I'd of wanted you here I'd of fetched you."

Lucinda said defiantly: "Since when have your wants become law for me?"

"When a man has an understandin'—"

"You've had no understanding with me, Ben Redcliff!"

Color whipped into the sheriff's raw cheeks. "Mebbe not with you proper," he managed to smile, "but you know mighty well your ol' man allowed—"

"My old man, as you call him, allows plenty but I doubt if he's got around to trading off his daughter. In any event," Cindy said, clear and cold, "I will pick my own man and if any trading is done *I* will do it."

Some of Redcliff's rage slipped out in a sneer. "Your ol' man lettin' you wear the pants now, is he?"

"You should know well enough who's been running that spread—"

"You mean Craftner?"

"Link Craftner's the ramrod. My father's the owner. But I'm the one that's been holding it together and mine is the judgment—"

"You showed damn pore judgment turnin' up at this shindy with a two-by-four drifter!"

Cindy smiled. "Stroud's not drifting. He's Three Sixes' new strayman and I think he will know stolen beef when he sees it."

A whiteness rolled over Ben Redcliff's raw face. He half lifted a hand as though minded to strike her. But he was a man of swift changes and he let the hand drop while his mind circled Stroud and tried to think where this led to.

But he could not be sure and so he thrust Stroud aside and reconsidered the girl. "If you're runnin' that outfit then I guess you're the one—" He let the rest of that go and looked at her carefully. "I'd like to see you outside—"

"Anything you've got to tell me can be said right here."

"You want this whole dang push to be knowin' your business?"

"The Lees have no secrets from the rest of this range."

"All right," the sheriff growled, "I will make myself plain. Three Sixes is a plucked goose an' everybody knows it. How long do you figger you'll be runnin' that spread if I step aside?"

"I've been weaned long enough to know which side of the bread your butter's on. Step anywhere you feel like," Cindy said with curling lips. "You're as hungry for plucked goose as any coyote in this country and if it gives you an appetite to lick Wafer's boots don't expect to find *me* pounding nails in your shirt tail."

The bright and wicked shining of the man's pale stare was more suggestive than words of the things going through his mind, yet he surprised Stroud again.

"Aw, now Cindy," he exclaimed in a wheedling kind of voice, "you're too smart to believe that. Your Daddy's the best friend I got—"

"Is that the reason you're always fetching whisky to Three Sixes?"

Redcliff brushed that aside. "What I'm talkin' about's this rustlin'. A man can't do only just so much —I mean if you had any proof—"

"I understand what you mean. You hate poison bad to see us keeping losing stock, but there's a limit to the scope of a sheriff's activities. You can't catch them at it and every time you're smart enough to get on their trail the tracks peter out or else they cross a county line and leave you bogged in red tape. If our boys get shot up it's too bad of course but if we can't get the names and addresses of the responsible parties there's just nothing you can do. You try to be helpful, but if we insist on shooting back and somebody gets a hole through him you'll have to drop the whole business because, as sheriff of this country, you can't afford to get mixed up in what some careless fool might describe as a 'range war.' Isn't that what you're trying to tell me?''

"No!" shouted Redcliff in a high half-strangled voice. "You know damn well that ain't what I'm tryin' to say!"

"What *are* you trying to say then? That if I won't play house you'll take your shiny star away and let Dan Wafer ruin us?"

Redcliff's outraged stare held the wildness of a stallion bronc's. He slammed one lightning look at Stroud and it seemed as though temper would set him crazy. But he still had his teeth in caution. It showed in the bunching muscles of his jaw as his sulphurous stare beat against Stroud's face and he said with the rasp of sand in his voice: "I suppose we've got *you* to thank for this. Mebbe you better step over to my office."

Stroud smiled thinly.

"Come on," Redcliff growled, starting toward him. "Get movin'."

"What for?"

"Never mind what for. Get goin'," the sheriff snarled.

"Aren't you forgettin' this is still a free country?"

"Free for responsible citizens. I don't put saddle bums in that class. Move out!"

"I guess not," Stroud said, and the strain in this room ran three degrees higher. It was like a cold breath blowing across Stroud's spine. This crowd was watching him even as the sheriff, trying to decide if he were hard as he looked.

He saw Ben Redcliff's problem, even sympathized with him in a detached sort of fashion. This girl had made the sheriff look like a fool; and he would indeed have been a fool if he had not guessed her defiance to have sprung from the presence of this stranger. Redcliff felt the need of some gesture. Many things a sheriff could ignore in this country but he could not continue living in the place without respect.

This was the corrosive eating away the sheriff's judgment. Need was a pressure steadily driving him toward violence and Stroud, watching his eyes, thought how stark and unchanging were the behavior patterns by which men lived.

Sweat cracked through Ben Redcliff's skin. Stroud correctly gauged his murderous impulse and, as the sheriff's hand drove hipward, he took one forward step and struck.

That blow rocked Redcliff's head like a mallet, the shock of it loosening all his bunched muscles. He went back on his heels clawing wildly for balance and Stroud's left fist plowed into his stomach.

An agonized groan tumbled out of the crowd and the sheriff's eyes looked like they would roll off his cheekbones. He was folding at the middle when Stroud's lifting right exploded against his jaw. And that was the end of it.

The sheriff went down like a rotten house.

Stroud felt no triumph. In all that room no one moved or spoke, and he saw how the golden shine of the lamps spread its pallid glow across that blank sea of faces. He knew he had been as big a fool as Ben Redcliff.

4

HANDS OFF

IN the eyes of this crowd he read his past and his future; it was that plain and simple. It was carved on those wooden faces, built into those motionless scarce-breathing shapes so meticulously still in the unstable quiet. It was a taste and an odor. The substance of death.

His glance shuttled round. The hush deepened. He understood what kind of men these were and that what he did now could make or break him, that these next few moments might color all his days; and the strain that had been the sheriff's undoing now put its full weight against him.

He laid his hands on his hips, all his thoughts turned forlorn and a part of his mind still wondering if it were yet too late to get out of this.

He could not know how hard a picture he made with the light striking off the tough planes of his cheeks.

The girl had her chin up but she wasn't sure now. It showed in her quickened breathing, in the harried exploratory slanch of her stare. Things were going too fast or too far for her program and, when her look whipped suddenly past him, something in the manner of it cocked Stroud's muscles.

She said through stiff lips: "Stick with me. I'm afraid—"

There was no time for more. The bunched shapes by the door were writhing apart and Stroud saw Dan Wafer plow through them, cutting a trail with his serge-coated shoulders.

Contempt touched his cheeks as he looked down at the sheriff. Then his lifting glance rummaged Cindy's white face and his bold eyes showed a brightening amusement.

"Hate to see a cute trick like you wastin' her talent with this kind of horseplay. These drifters ain't the answer to your problem."

"You framed the problem. I guess you should know."

Wafer grinned. "You want to keep Three Sixes. All this guy will do is complicate matters. Just another cheap crook tryin' to dodge posse bullets or hunt up a place to hide out from a rope. When the goin' gets rough you'll see him fade for the hills. Why don't you get smart?" he said gruffly.

She did not at once answer but stood silent, considering him. Stroud could see her scornful look gnawing into the man, turning him unsure and cutting behind his show of amused tolerance.

He said irritably: "Way you're goin' someone's liable to get hurt."

"If you don't want someone hurt why don't you call off your rustlers?"

Wafer managed a laugh. He even made it sound reasonable, though Stroud thought to catch the rasp of buried anger back of it. "That was funny as hell the first time you pulled it, but why not stick to the facts? That brother of yours knows a heap— Well, let it ride. If you've made up your mind I'm back of all your troubles you should know a better way to get them stopped than hiring gun hands."

"The idea of gun hands on Three Sixes worries you?"

Wafer grinned derisively. "Nothin' worries me. I just don't like to see you mixin' with riffraff—"

"Rodding a crew of drifters and range bums doesn't appear to have done your credit much damage."

He said, brusque with his answer: "I have to hire a tough crew to protect my interests."

"And why do you think I'm trying to hire one?"

"Different with you. Women slung together like you are don't need no gun to get her way with a man."

Cindy looked at him carefully. "Are you by any chance suggesting that I marry you?"

Stroud, silently watching, observed the conscious power of this big smiling ranchman, the overmastering pride which gave the deep-tanned intelligent face of the man its aggressive aliveness and rugged masculine appeal. His confident assurance had obviously been founded on the solid bedrock of demonstrable performance.

Now he was chuckling, showing his dimples, cornering Cindy with a glance of approval. "Always said you was smart. Be the best insurance against rustlers you could have." He said with bold impudence, "There's a preacher up at Mallart—"

There was a touch of hysteria in Cindy's sudden laugh. "A robber king's bride!" Then unutterable scorn flashed out of her voice. "I wouldn't marry you, Dan, if there wasn't anything left but halfwits and cripples—I would sooner bed down with an out-and-out polecat!"

Wafer's shape turned still. One moment of breathless silence followed, then his smile narrowed down and got ugly and a high roan flush rolled across his tight cheeks. He said: "I hope you won't have to eat those words," and, turning, clouted a man from his path and strode down a widening lane toward the door.

CINDY clutched Stroud's arm. "Was I wrong? I was mad to defy him, but—"

"You wanted it that way, didn't you?"

Her glance searched his face. "I suppose I did . . ."

"Then leave it alone." He said, "Never look back."

A racket of excited talk broke out and all over the room men moved out of their tracks and spoke too loud in their release from tension.

"Come on," Stroud said, "let's get out of this place," and guided her north along the line of packed benches. He didn't see Redcliff.

The caller jumped up on his box again. Fiddles scraped and he called through the din: *"Grab yo' self some Texas Star!"*

Halfway down the hall Cindy stopped. "Wait," she said. "I think perhaps we'd better use the back door."

Stroud swept her a look of sardonic amusement. "Make up your mind. If you're playin' this straight you don't want the back door. Never lead with your chin and then start hedgin'. If you want to make a bluff stick you've got to go through with it."

"I don't want to get you killed."

He gave her a tough grin.

"They may be laying for you—"

"Good time to find out."

"You mean you're taking that job? You're throwing in with Three Sixes?"

"Ain't that what you told Wafer?"

Color crept into her cheeks. "I can't hold you to that."

"Wafer can."

She didn't get it right away. When she caught the whole meaning of his words she looked astonished, concerned. "I wasn't aiming to trap you. I wanted to worry him," she said. "I didn't think about—"

"That's over and done with."

"But you don't have to stay. You can climb on your horse and—"

"You can't scoop spilled milk back into the bucket."

"It wouldn't help any for me to say that I'm sorry. I don't know that I am. We could use you, Mike. We'd be mighty glad to get you. Would you consider signing on at one hundred and fifty a month?"

Stroud looked at her sharply. "Gun fighter wages. Just what are you trying to buy with that money?"

She was watching him closely, studying him, still probing to turn up his real worth and character.

"Loyalty."

"Must come pretty steep in these parts."

"I haven't found any, yet." She said quietly, "I'll not try to pretend we've much hope of holding out, or that this rustling is the size of it. This stealing is just a means to an end—it's not the only one they're using.

They're working on my brother, on me, on my father; it's been going on for months.

"I sometimes wonder if it hasn't been going on right from the beginning. When my father, Cyrano Lee, first came into this country he saw what he wanted and went to work to get it. This was a great range in those days; grass all over—the old-timers say it was belly-high on a horse. Dad was rough-handed, more sure of what he wanted and more determined to get it than the outfits he displaced."

She paused a moment, reflecting. "One of the men he broke was Dan Wafer's father. They owned the Bar Dash then and it controlled a lot of water. After they lost it Dan's father shot himself. Dan has never forgiven us."

"Where's he gettin' all his weight?"

"He's pretty well fixed, got a big outfit now. He quit Thief River after they lost the Bar Dash. He came back with a little bunch of cattle three years ago and bought out a couple of homesteaders at the edge of the pine breaks north of the river. His cows weren't much to look at but they multiplied faster than jackrabbits. Last November he took over the Cross Triangle and brought in some outside riders; he didn't hire them to punch cattle. In January he took over the next closest outfit and began crowding the Boxed Circle. Two months ago they sold out to him and that put him right up against our north and east boundaries."

"Where does Redcliff fit in?"

She shook her head. "I don't know. Dad was thrown from a horse and hurt his back last year. It paralyzed his legs. Ben's been keeping him in whisky."

"How far out is your place?"

"Eight miles. Will your horse go that far?"

"We'll find out," Stroud said, starting her toward the door.

"Mike, I'm afraid we'll run into trouble out there. Let's go—"

"You'll never lick trouble by dodging it."

He loosened the gun in his holster, nodding when the men round the doorway made room for them. "What did you say was the name of your range boss?"

"Link Craftner."

"That the feller we saw talkin' to Wafer?"

"Yes."

"How long's he been with you?"

"Just since Dad's been laid up. Lockett, our former ramrod, quit to take over a job at Tubac."

Stroud nodded. "Wait here."

He stepped into the yard, making no effort to hide his identity. He stopped under the lantern hung above the hall's entrance and rolled a smoke left-handed and lighted it. No shots rang out, no one approached him, nothing happened. He had judged it would probably be this way. They hadn't quite made up their minds about him; or Dan Wafer hadn't, which was likely the same thing.

He was not fooled into thinking he had anyone buffaloed. He knew this country's ways and its people and too much smoke had crossed his trail for him to put any stock in present lack of attention. Every man in that hall had marked him well. He was going to be watched. Nor did he attribute this to his appearance with the girl, to his tussle with the sheriff or to Cindy's declaration that Three Sixes was hiring him. These could prove to be contributory causes but he would have been a marked man in any event; it was in the very nature of this town's location. Most of these men had drifted here from other places and would regard with suspicion every stranger who came near them.

He stood watching the night with eyes bleakly narrowed above his reticent cheeks. With stubborn jaw and sandy hair he was a man to remember, and therein lay his quandary. There were scars on his body and you didn't have to see them to know they were there. He had that look, that indefinable brand of the bravo, stamped indelibly into his features. He looked at home in this place because he was at home in it, veteran of a hundred towns like it, understanding what made it function.

He stood with his back against the front of the building. A chill wind rolled off the rain-wet mountains and distant crags cut black shapes out of the moon brightened sky.

Stroud pitched away his half finished cigarette, seeing the bright shower of sparks where it struck. He hitched up his gun belt and strode through the shadows and said to the man he found standing by his horse: "You had your chance and passed it up, so you weren'ᵗ waitin' here to pot me. What *are* you waitin' for?"

"You got the wrong slant on this. I want to give you some advice—"

"I haven't asked for your advice."

"Nevertheless," Redcliff said, "I ain't in the habit of shootin' settin' ducks. You were lucky a while ago. Take my advice and pull your freight."

"All right," Stroud said. "I've been warned. Now draw or drag."

"Just a minute," the sheriff breathed. Reaching

forward he flipped back Stroud's cowhide vest. He had his quick look and pulled himself out of range. "Just what I thought!" he cried hoarsely; and his face, now in light, showed the full measure of his malevolence.

"You've spoke your piece," Stroud drawled. "I'll speak mine. If you don't want a hole through that star keep away from me."

5

DRESSED TO KILL

SHOVING past Redcliff, he untied the two horses, mounted his own and led the girl's black to the door of the hall.

Cindy came out and got into her saddle. She unlashed her slicker and slipped it on against the increasing chill whipping down off the mountains, and swung onto the rain-wet road, heading west.

"This Craftner," Stroud said, riding along beside her. "Aside from what he's said do you know anything about him?"

The girl shook her head. "He claims to have known Lockett before Lockett came to Three Sixes. He told us Lockett had written him there was a vacancy here and that, if we hadn't gotten anyone suitable, he'd be glad of the job. He seemed capable enough so Dad hired him."

"Without checking?"

"I wrote Lockett at Tubac."

"Lockett know him?"

"I've never heard from Lockett."

Stroud chewed on that in silence for a while, considering the beauty of this moonlit range and observing how the packed road followed the convolutions of the river. "Had much drought in this country?"

"This is the first rain we've had in eleven months."

"I was thinkin' about this river. Brush shows high water mark a foot above the banks. That's a flash flood mark, I reckon. But the thing don't make sense. River's cut a channel eighty feet across with a bed twenty feet below the level of the banks, yet there's barely a trickle after an all-day rain an' what pools I've seen look like stagnant water."

"Yes."

The argent light playing over full breast and rounded thigh unsettled the run of his thoughts and sharpened hungers that were better forgotten. Vingie had been lush and provocative, too; and Stroud cursed beneath his breath with remembrance.

"Yes," Cindy said with unexpected harshness, "a sign of the Wafer blight on this land. Overgrazing has left its curse on this range and the Lees have had their share in it, but two years ago there was feed through here for a thousand cattle. Ten couldn't graze it now the year around. This was OBT range; they've gone out of business since Wafer threw a dam across the river ten miles north. With diverted water he has made himself a chain of fourteen lakes." She said with a fierce bottled anger: "One acre of Stirrup will carry a cow all year."

"And they let him get away with it?"

"He *got* away with it. There were five or six men killed. Three outfits went broke and the Cross Triangle sold out to him."

Stroud said out of a long silence, "What's the dam done to your place?"

"We've been able to get by. We've got two creeks that cut down from up above it. We've got five tanks—six, in fact, but one of them's no good. We haven't been hit as hard as most of the ranches round here. He'll be picking up some of them any day now."

"Why not beat him to it? Why not pick them up yourself?"

"What would we use for money? We haven't sold a cow this year. We gathered two beef herds and had them stampeded—"

"Slap a mortgage on the place."

"We've got a mortgage on it now and—"

"How many hands on your payroll?"

"Six, counting Craftner."

"Cow hands or drifters?"

"You can't get any cow hands to buck Dan Wafer."

"Will your drifters buck him?"

She shrugged her shoulders wearily. "Your guess is as good as mine. At least they haven't quit yet. We're paying gun wages. They'll probably hang around until we run out of money."

"Have you got enough stuff left to make up a herd?"

She held herself still but there was excitement in her voice. "A trail herd? I think so. Might take us two weeks to make the gather." She looked at him again. She brought her horse up closer and put a hand on his arm and that contact was enormously stirring. "If I thought I could trust you—"

He said harshly: "Trust no man with anything."

She drew back from him, startled. He read disappointment into her look, and wonder, and something else he could not so easily define. Remembrance abruptly changed her expression and he understood that what had been left of that moment's fragment of melody was gone. Her glance met and locked with his again and she cried vehemently, "I can't be like that! And I have got to have help. I'm not going to let them take Three Sixes away from me if I can find any way to prevent it. I've got to trust *some*one."

"Then you're a fool," he said, unaccountably angry, and reined his horse away from her.

They rode the next four miles without speaking. They were into the hills now and steadily climbing toward the northern ramparts of the valley. This road was become little better than a wagon rut encroached as often as not on both sides by brush. The river lay far to the left of them now and, looking that way, Stroud observed a distant cluster of lights which he guessed would be Stirrup. They would soon be in timber and the air had a bite to it which emphasized the hollow ring of the horses' hoofs whenever their shoes struck stone.

Stroud said abruptly: "Your father got any brothers?"

"One."

"He live around here?"

"No." Cindy's tone was reserved and drawn away from him now. "I believe he's supposed to be somewhere in California."

"How long since you've seen him?"

"I never have. He left this country before I was born."

"Write pretty regular, does he?"

"We haven't heard from him in years."

She wasn't asking any questions on her own hook. Still riled, he reckoned. He said, "How big of a crew has Stirrup got?"

"Around eighteen men."

Stroud stared. "Ain't that a little unusual?"

"Stirrup," she said dryly, "is an unusual outfit. Its crew has a lot of riding to do—but that needn't worry you." A faint contempt edged into her tone and the look she gave him had no friendliness in it. "There's a cutoff ahead that will take you to Globe."

"Your way of sayin' you've changed your mind?"

"No. The offer's still open. I'm in no position to be so particular." She said bitterly: "I would hire an escaped lifer if I thought he might help me to save Three Sixes."

Stroud showed her the shine of his teeth and she said, "You don't stack up much different from the rest of our payroll. You're running from something."

"Maybe not." He smiled lazily. "I might be a hard working stage robber sizing things up for a new base of operations."

"No stage comes within fifty miles of Thief River."

"What's fifty miles to an ambitious stage stopper?"

"Just get this straight," she said coldly. "Your past doesn't interest me, nor your reasons for being here. I'm hiring you to do a job and as long as you do it I will have no complaint."

"You would stand off the law for me?"

There was dislike in her eyes when she looked at him then. But she didn't dodge the issue. "I will do what I can."

"Fair enough," Stroud said, and looked at her steadily. "I'll stick around for awhile. As your strayman. When the job doesn't suit me I will go somewhere else."

They rode on, climbing deeper into the timber and

through it. The higher peaks loomed closer, black and stark against the stars. A lonely land, primitive and turbulent; a land where men's passions could be given full rein. A land steeped in violence.

Breaking through the dark tangle of his thoughts, the girl said, "We're about there. You've been riding our range for the past half hour. When we top this ridge you'll be seeing headquarters."

She had the appearance of wanting to say something additional but turned away without doing so, eyes thoughtfully locked between her black gelding's ears, lithe shape swaying forward in the saddle as she helped him up the difficult trail.

Stroud, following her, thought again of how completely this girl could be the answer to some man's reason for existence. Then they were cresting the ridge, staring across an argent expanse of moonlit bench that ran flat as a table to a far stand of pine. Cindy said with clear pride: "Three Sixes."

Stroud saw a clutter of paintless buildings centered by the low solid bulk of a ranch house. Like the corrals it was built of peeled logs and looked rugged. No lights showed from the two-foot apertures which did service as windows; no lights showed anywhere, which was not surprising on a working cow ranch at the hour of midnight.

It was something else which narrowed Stroud's eyes and quickened his pulses.

He always noticed a definite feeling about places and he didn't like the feeling he had about this one. There was something odd here, something wrong, something stealthy. Quiet and serene though it looked in the moonlight there was an undercurrent of tenseness about it, an intangible aura of evil or suspicion or excitement, an electric quality strangely at variance with its somnolent appearance.

Growing more and more dissatisfied, he sent a baffled stare prowling the alternate patches of black shadow and silver. Had he made a mistake in coming here? Over the years his reflexes had been too carefully cultivated for him not to put stock in his hunches. Hunches were a manifestation of instinct and so long as a man trusted instinct he was safe. Luck ran out—as a lot of dim shapes in his past could testify. He'd had the breaks up till now but he hadn't much liked this job from the first.

He slanched a look at the girl. She had pulled up her horse and was waiting for him with her eyes big and dark and questioning. He moved the roan abreast of her. "What is it?" she whispered; and something blurred across the far edge of his vision, scraping his nerves like a file on tin. There was a man over there in the shadows with a rifle.

A low call sailed out of those shadows. Cindy twisted her head. "Dreen! What's happened?"

"Round back of the barn. Who's that you got with you?"

"New hand," she said and put her horse into motion.

Stroud trailed her past the dark gallery which stretched full length across the front of the house. A barn loomed up looking a little neglected, but commodious and durable like everything else he had seen about this place. He followed her into the gloom beyond the barn's far side and came into bright moonlight again at the back where three silent men stood around a held horse.

Three sixes were burned on the animal's left hip and a man was tied face down across the saddle. His eyes were wide open but they weren't telling him anything.

Cindy's cheeks were haggard. "It's—it's Curly, isn't it?"

The tallest of the trio nodded. "Ol' Dunny here just fetched him in. He's got a hole in his chest you could drive a team through."

And the shortest man said, "Craftner put him to ridin' the east fence this mawnin'."

The east fence, Stroud remembered, bordered one of the outfits taken over by Stirrup.

The three men were watching him with looks of suspicion.

The girl saw this; she tried to pull herself together. "This is Mike Stroud. He'll be riding as strayman. Stroud, meet Shampoo Charlie, Banjo Bill and Chuck Murgatroyd."

No one nodded or offered to shake hands. Charlie was the tall one, a loose jointed misfit standing six foot five with a cadaverous cast of countenance and gangling arms that reached almost to his kneecaps. Banjo was the shortest, a pallid faced dwarf with a hunch on his back and coarse gray hair on the backs of his fingers. The third man, Murgatroyd, was a thickset albino with two guns strapped about his solid middle.

Riffraff. Stroud had met their kind in a hundred camps. Saddle bums. Men without ties and very few scruples. Diverse as they were in physical appearance, a sameness stamped them all, a hard wariness of eye and a fondness for keeping their hands near their pistols.

Stroud watched them over the cigarette he was rolling and wondered what form their suspicion would take.

The tall one scuffed a boot. He looked at Banjo and then at Cindy.

"You been expectin' company? Relatives, mebbe?"

Cindy shook her head.

"Well, you got some. Ol' man an' a girl—pretty flossy. Give the name of Lee. Come two-three hours ago."

"In a buggy," Benjo added.

Murgatroyd nodded. "We put the buggy in the barn."

By her look the news didn't mean much to Cindy; then all at once the whole expression of her face changed and she looked sharply at Stroud. She was remembering that question he had asked about uncles and he didn't think she was liking it much.

She got out of the saddle, tossing her reins at Banjo. To Stroud she said, "I'll see you in the morning," and went off around the barn in the direction of the house.

Stroud got out of his saddle and discovered the three were still watching him. Not with the surly sniff-and-growl suspicion habitual with their kind but with the concentrated savagery of wolves smelling blood.

"An' how would *you* be knowin' about Three Sixes' company?"

That was Murgatroyd, the albino, stepping clear of the others to give himself room.

Stroud brought a match up the seam of his Levis and touched its flame to the end of his quirly, considering where this placed him. He dragged the smoke deep into his lungs and let it out through his nostrils, lips lengthening and tightening. No one needed to tell him he was walking on eggs or that a wrong move here would wind up in gun smoke. Sometimes toughness paid off, but there were times when it didn't.

"I bumped into them coming into town," he said.

"An' they told you all their business, I guess!"

"What's your angle?"

"I like to know where I am on a job. I like to know what kind of galoots I got round me. It seems uncommon odd to me, by God, that you an' them both should turn up on the night Curly Gaines comes home tied onto his saddle!"

Stroud's smile stretched out, thin and cold. He said nothing.

A slow, wicked breathing lifted and lowered the burly arch of Murgatroyd's chest; the deep red of his pupils grew brighter and brighter. The corrosive of doubt was boiling inside him, burning away the thin guards of his caution. He said: "I think, by God, Stirrup's plantin' a spy!"

6

THE STATUS QUO

BANJO'S mouth corners tightened. Shampoo Charlie tipped his bony shoulders forward and a feeling of something expected reshaped his gaunt cheeks in a remote kind of smiling.

Stroud, considering these things, let go of the roan's reins and crowded Murgatroyd into taking one backward step. "And what do you propose to do about it?"

The albino's eyes rounded, not liking what he saw. But he wasn't running from it, either. "When I see a snake I generally tear its damn head off."

"And when you see a spy?"

"He'll go back to Stirrup tied onto his saddle the same way Curly come back to us!"

Stroud said, "Killed with words, I reckon. Let me give you some advice. Never start anything you aren't able to finish."

Murgatroyd studied him, darkly hating him. "Don't feel so proud—an' don't be foolin' yourself. I'll finish it all right if I make up my mind to."

"If you're afraid," Stroud said, "pull out of this."

They stood less than four feet apart and the albino's hate flew across that space like a gust of hot wind.

It wouldn't take much to crowd this man into gunplay. Stroud said, "What's botherin' you?"

"I don't want you around."

"You the boss of this outfit?"

"I can take over—"

"If you can," Stroud said, "it's no wonder this spread is headed for the dogs. Now I've had enough gab. Put up or shut up."

Murgatroyd twisted his lips in a grin. "I expect I made a mistake about you. You'll find the bunkhouse over there next the corrals."

That broke the play up. The tall and gangling Charlie loosened his shoulders and the hunchback, Banjo Bill, asked dourly, "What we goin' to do about Curly?"

"Bury him," Stroud said, thus taking the initiative away from Murgatroyd and, by that much, further damaging the man's reputation. "I'll leave you boys to take care of it."

Picking up the roan's reins he strode off toward the corrals.

WHEN he walked up to the bunkhouse minutes later the place was dark and appeared to be deserted. But Stroud knew better than to judge by appearances. He would as soon have worked with a pack of curs as with this flotsam the girl had assembled. She used these men because she had to, but it wasn't in them to pay off kindness with any coin save contempt. Cunning as coyotes, chancy as snakes, they were spawned of a breed answering nothing but the whip and it was probably an intimate knowledge of their ways which had raised the albino to straw boss under Craftner.

And what kind of a ruffian was Craftner?

He brushed the thought aside, knowing the futility of trying to base an action on the sands of speculation. Nothing but facts could serve him here and his concern right now was with the crew, not the range boss. He'd called Murgatroyd's bluff but nothing had been resolved. All life was a cycle, a pattern of sequences as fixed and immutable as the transcribed course of a walking beam. Cause and effect as precise and unvarying as the result of dropping a stone into water. First the splash and then the ripples.

The bunkhouse door, like both its windows, stood open. Stepping inside he took a quick look around. The room was oblong with the windows cut into its north and south ends and a scarred plank table in its center.

There were four tiers of bunks, three bunks to a tier, two tiers to a side with clothing hung from pegs between them. The door was centered in the cabin's east wall, bunks at either side and no space left at the ends. By the nature of this arrangement these two tiers were nearer the windows than the pair across the table. But a single bunk in each of these tiers showed use, the rest of the crew bunking against the west wall.

By deciding which window caught prevailing winds Stroud made up his mind which bunk would be Murgatroyd's. Ripping off the bedding he spread his own roll in its place. If there was going to be trouble it might as well come now.

He kicked the torn-up bed out into the aisle. Draped his shell belt over a peg set into the frame of the bunk above, leaving the heavy .45 in its holster. He took off his vest and hung it over the belt and put his shirt over that. Wearing boots and pants, he stretched out on the bunk and waited.

He did not have to wait long. Within a half hour he heard the crew approaching. They weren't doing much talking. Probably had it all settled.

He watched the men file in, Murgatroyd in the lead. He could see their black shapes limned against the far window. He saw Murgatroyd stop. Heard his sudden sharp breath.

The silence became electric.

Distrust and suspicion boiled up like a smell. The coyote way, Stroud reflected. The anger would come later. Right now they were stalled in the clutch of suspicion; it was a rankness in Murgatroyd's voice when he said:

"You have a heavy hand, friend. What are you trying to do here?"

"Just makin' a little room for myself."

"Couldn't you find an empty bunk?"

"I like a breeze with my sleepin'—"

"That bunk belongs to me."

"Tough," Stroud said. "Go think yourself into another one."

Murgatroyd stood very still. He had really only two choices. He could jump Stroud now and take his chances or he could take another bunk and lose the last of the hold he had over this crew.

Stroud never doubted which the man would do. He was caught flat-footed in the same predicament which had earlier trapped the furious Ben Redcliff.

But there was a lot of cold blood in Murgatroyd's veins. He had a much better hold on his temper than the sheriff and the salutary advantage of a previous experience.

He held himself still, burly shoulders cocked. "Have our trails crossed before?"

"Look," Stroud said in the manner of a man whose patience is exhausted. "I liked this bunk and I took it. There are eleven others here, six of 'em empty—not countin' the dead man's. If none of those suit you go on outside and bed down with the broncs."

"I think—"

"Climb into a bunk or get the hell out!"

The man's control was incredible. Stroud could feel his stare beating through the pale gloom, malign as the gaze of a hooded snake, but his silhouetted shoulders stayed as still as the door posts.

Stroud sat up, booted feet to the floor. "Charlie," he said, "strike a match to that lamp!"

There was a shift in the sound of someone's breathing. The gangling giant, shuffling forward, ignited a match and, leaning across one end of the table, lifted the chimney from the lamp that was there. He brought the match forward, sent flame raveling across the turned-up wick.

Grotesque shadows rocked along the log walls. But the light wasn't needed. Murgatroyd was gone.

THE cook's call to breakfast pulled Stroud from his bunk an hour before daylight. The hunchback was the only one in sight and, already dressed, he was cleaning his sixshooter.

Stroud yawned, got up and reached for his hat. Tightening his belt he stamped into his boots, afterwards pausing to dig out his Durham. While rolling his smoke he considered the hunchback who gave no evidence of discerning this interest.

With his fire going good Stroud got into his shirt, stuffed in its tails and put on his vest. Banjo Bill, by this time, had finished operations and slipped his gun back in leather. Tossing his oil rags at an empty bunk he said, still without looking in Stroud's direction, "Keep your eye peeled fer squalls," and departed.

Before buckling on his cartridge belt Stroud thoughtfully checked the loads in his pistol. Then he found the water tub and performed his "ablutions," slicking back rebellious hair with his fingers.

When he stepped into the cookshack the rest were eating. He reckoned the man at the table's head to be Craftner. One place was still vacant, the dead man's, he guessed; and dropped onto the bench without remark.

Dreen, the man whose hail had stopped Stroud last night, was an unshaven man with a patch on a string tied over his right eye. He nodded at Stroud and called to the cook for another cup of java. The cook was a halfbreed Papago Indian answering to the name of "Go Slow."

The range boss was a lantern-jawed man in batwing chaps decorated with conchas and a gambler's striped vest over a shirt whose sleeve supports looked to have come off the legs of some harpy. He had a tight thin mouth. "Stroud? I'm Craftner. When you get done they want you up to the house."

He picked his teeth with a match stick and went out, the crew straggling after him. Murgatroyd, the last to get his pants off the bench, stood inscrutably waiting until he got Stroud's attention. Even then he dabbled, with his thoughts working through him and his queer red eyes still doggedly laboring over Stroud's tough features.

"Well?" Stroud said.

The two-gun man looked hardly satisfied yet but, after a further combing of his mental range, declared, "When you rode in here last night I put you down for another of these sorry jackals that're forever taggin' round from hell to breakfast hirin' out their irons to the highest bidder. It was a bad mistake—"

"If you made it," Stroud smiled. "I don't think you did."

Murgatroyd's mouth creased through the smoke of his quirly. He took a last drag and spun the butt through a window.

Stroud shoved back from the table. "Where you made your mistake was in thinkin' you could bluff me."

Murgatroyd said irritably, "You have to keep trompin' my toes?"

"Depends where you put 'em. Your slick little speech ain't foolin' me a particle. You've got a fouled-up backtrail you're tryin' to cut loose of. When I blew in here last night it was the first thing you thought about. You figured maybe you could bluff me into haulin' my freight. When that misfired you began to do some thinkin'. You done a pile of it, I reckon. You ain't sure about me yet."

Murgatroyd sneered. "An' a mind reader, too!"

"I can read *your* mind without trying. Somewhere back along the line you got some decent girl in trouble and you're tryin' to decide where I fit into that picture."

Murgatroyd's cheeks showed the shine of sweat.

"Generally," Stroud went on, "when a man's tryin' to lose himself he heads for the brush and does a heap of fast travelin'. He ain't honin' to be involved in no range feud. But a feller that will do one decent girl dirt ain't goin' to have no compunctions about repeating the performance.

"When you rode into Thief River you found the same setup I found. A whoppin' big outfit with its back to the wall and nothing holdin' it together but one damn pretty woman, hardly more than a kid, who probably couldn't tell a skunk from a house cat."

Murgatroyd's tongue rasped across dry lips. He stared without speaking over a long stretch of thinking, at last saying dustily, "You gunnin' for me?"

Stroud said, "If you don't like trouble don't go lookin' for it," and, moving past him, wheeled into the yard.

The sun was five minutes above a sawtoothed horizon, flushing the ridgetops with a golden glory and transforming the depressions into pools of mauve shadow. Swinging toward the house Stroud saw a girl round its corner, a well-made girl in a sage-colored dress clasping her tightly at breast and waist in the fashion of the time. Stepping out of the lavender shadow of the gallery the sudden change to full sunlight made her close her eyes. Puzzled and a little curious, Stroud took advantage of this to consider her more thoroughly.

She was half a hand taller than Cindy and did not have Cindy's bronzed outdoor look. She was a well-filled-out girl with the blue-black luster of midnight hair massed above a wide forehead, above a grave and serene face that had its own quiet distinction.

She caught the sound of his approach and opened her eyes. They were proud and a little guarded yet met his inspection without shyness, directly, as a man's would. Color touched her cheeks, more decidedly tinting them as he let the silence run on without speaking.

She said without inflection: "Were you looking for someone?"

"Not exactly," he answered, dragging off his battered hat. "I'm the strayman. Was told I'm wanted at the house—would you know about that?"

Something queerly alert briefly slid through her look and was gone without tracks. "The office," she said, "is at the end of the gallery."

There was melody in her voice, the hint of something strong and maturely emotional, deep as still water, below the quiet surface. Her lips, long and pleasant, lazily turned up a smile which broadened to become more personal as her glance, still reserved, more directly considered him. "You'll be Stroud, the one they've been talking about."

"Reckon you've pegged me, ma'am. Bet Duke's Mixture to Durham you're the district's new schoolmarm—"

An edge of bright laughter danced through her look. "You lose the Duke's Mixture. I'm Lucinda's cousin, Beulah May, from Tonopah—" Breaking off and half turning, her glance lifting past him, she called: "Here I am, darling—over here by the stray man."

Cindy stood without movement at the edge of the gallery. She looked swiftly at the girl and as quickly back to Stroud, her lips tightening. "The strayman has work to do and Uncle Tal's mislaid his—"

"Poor old Dad." Beulah May shook her head and went back around the corner.

Cindy's glance dug into Stroud. "What's the trouble between you and Murgatroyd?"

"Did he say there was any trouble?"

"The suggestion came from Craftner. He has told my father you're a bad influence here. He has let it be known he considers you a spy in the employ of Stirrup."

"Murgatroyd's song. That tie in with your notion?"

"I don't know what to think. I keep recalling last night, seeing Craftner in those shadows with Dan Wafer. I keep recalling, too, that it was you who warned me not to trust—"

"It's still good advice."

Her eyes turned dark and round and urgent. "Would you rod this outfit if the job were offered you?"

"You mean step into Craftner's boots? I guess not."

"Why not? Are you afraid?"

Stroud studied his hands and tipped a look at her obliquely. "It isn't that."

"What is it, then?"

"If you don't trust Craftner, why not give him more rope?"

"I haven't the time. We had to mortgage this place to keep operating. It's been all we could do to keep up the interest—"

"Who holds your paper?"

"A Phoenix commission house. The note comes due sixty days from tomorrow. If they refuse to extend it—"

"You better round up some beef."

"I took that up with Craftner and Dad this morning. Craftner's against it. He reminded me of what happened to the other two herds we tried to trail. He says we'd never get it through."

Stroud's reticent stare roved over to the corrals where the range boss was giving out the day's riding orders. "What's bein' done about that dead guy, Curly?"

She spread her hands.

"Craftner know about this note?"

"Of course." Some of the worry juning through her boiled up into her eyes and suspicion crept into the long look she gave him. "Last night you asked if Dad had any brothers. It struck me at the time as a queer sort of question—"

"And now that the question has become significant it's opened your mind to a lot of dark notions."

"A lot of things naturally occur to me."

He grinned at her thinly. When he made no attempt to dissolve her suspicions, Cindy cried in full temper: "You don't care what I think, do you!"

He considered her in silence, finally saying with a shrug, "No mystery about it. On the trail south of town I met a man in a buggy. A woman was with him. She asked if I could tell them how to get to Thief River. We swapped half a dozen words. Man passed me a bottle, called the stuff *Lee's Elixir*. I remembered the name ridin' out here last night."

He saw the stiffness fall out of her shoulders and knew that she wanted to believe him. With her grass-green eyes and that corn-yellow hair she was a damned handsome filly, and the look of her now suddenly quickened his pulses, something brash and powerful and unsettling running between them like summer lightning.

He half reached out a hand, and her arms came up and crossed her breasts. "Mike, I'm scared."

"Your father recognize this feller?"

"It's been so long," she said, "since he left here . . . I don't see how he could. But Dad seems to accept him, calls him 'Tal' all the time and he talks about things Dad remembers. Things that happened here in the old days—little personal things like the names of favorite horses, people they knew, what Lizzie Gorham wore—"

"Say what fetched him back?"

She shook her head. "I have wondered. He says Tonopah's played out. I think he hopes to get Dad to put some money in his Elixir. He doesn't understand that we are down to rock bottom."

Stroud watched the crew riding off about their chores. "How are you figurin' to pay these gun hands?"

"We've a little cash, enough to meet our next payroll. After that I don't know."

"Can't you patch it up with Wafer? Give him back the Bar Dash—"

"I offered to do that. He just laughed at me."

"Must feel pretty cocky."

"He does, and he's got reason. You would understand better if you had lived around here. I used to feel sorry, a little guilty about Dan; he got dealt a stacked hand according to his way of figuring. But one raw deal doesn't make a man turn wolf without at heart he is more than half wolf already. He's a wolf all the way, smart and cunning and ruthless.

"I used to think my father was a pretty high-handed man, but that was before I understood the things back of it. Dad didn't originate this Thief River sequence; it was an old story here when Dad played out his hand. When he came into this region the Bar Dash was top dog, an outfit built on the bones of ruined ranchers, financed by loot taken over at gunpoint and run by a man who had gone power crazy—Dan's father, Long Tom Wafer."

She said in a voice that locked away her own feelings, "These are feuding hills and I guess they always will be. Generosity and faith and fair-dealing are scorned aliens. This was an outlaws' paradise when my father came here. He had a little cash, a lot of cold nerve and a little more vision than the broken men he found in this country. He showed them what organization could do for them, banded them together and set out to wreck Wafer. He did it. He shared out the spoils with the men who had helped him and later, one by one, he bought those men out and wound up with Three Sixes. That's the long and the short of it. Naturally he made some enemies. A few of those men, like Ben Redcliff, are still around."

"Includin' Dan Wafer."

Cindy nodded.

"And he's bent on getting back in the saddle."

"Of course. He intends to stay there this time. He stood right here two months ago and bragged he would beggar every outfit in these hills."

"You think he's bought Redcliff?"

"A lot of men have bought Ben's star. He's never bothered to play sheriff outside the town limits."

"You mean he wouldn't help Wafer?"

"Ben never lets prejudice keep his hand away from an easy dollar. He'll help anyone who uses the right kind of bait, but only if he believes he is helping himself more."

"What about these other people?"

"You won't find one man who will lift a finger. They're still scraping meals from their last bowl of pottage."

She put up a hand as Stroud would have spoken. "You're dealing with men who've been used before. The past is too much with them. In their experience all cattle barons are crooks. They figure last time they swapped the witch for the devil. If they got into it again they'd be inclined to side with Wafer—but they won't get into it. They can't see beyond their noses; they regard this as a showdown between Three Sixes and Stirrup. If things get too tough they'll crawl into their holes—"

"And let Dan Wafer bury them?"

"You'll never make them see that, Mike—"

Stroud's short laugh cut through her words. "At least," he said, "you've got that straight."

"You're running out?"

"I'll do what I hired on to do. If you want to play Joan of Arc, go ahead. But don't count on me to shoulder your grief."

7

NO ROOM AT THE WAGON

SHE stood, stiffly straight, with her green eyes watching him unreadably. She was quiet with the sharpest kind of knowledge; yet now, as earlier, he must have sensed in her a confusion of contradictions.

A kind of sadness crept through her glance and wistfulness reshaped her cheeks and she seemed in that moment completely alone.

Last night she had made him an unspoken offer or, at least, the suggestion had been in the air. It had taken him to that dance in her company and involved him in things which were near to her heart. Had it given her the courage to face Ben Redcliff?

Last night he had thought so; now he was not sure. Last night he'd been witched by the magnetism of a bewildering personality, caught up in the flight of her fancy, drugged with the promise of what she could bring a man; and she was letting him see these things again when anger flung up its bright curtain, closing him out like a bolted door.

"I thought I could depend on you."

"Don't make me responsible for your thoughts,"

Stroud cried; and she watched him tramp across the yard.

She listened to him walk away and her lips went tight and something new came into her eyes. She hung there a moment as though not quite sure, and Craftner stepped out of the bunkhouse with a coil of frayed rope in the grip of his hand.

She noticed how the breeze fluttered the scarf at his throat and the last look of softness went out of her face. She waited till the range boss tipped up his head. She lifted her chin then and beckoned.

Craftner came up with his look hard and probing. He waited her out, a man of forty or more, turned dark by weather and with his fund of self-confidence vaguely disturbed.

Lucinda said, "You needn't bother any more about that trail herd I mentioned."

"Glad to see you takin' in a few facts. Like I told your father, we ain't got enough man power to shove a herd through and we need every hand we can get to ride fence—"

"You won't have to worry any more about that."

A bank of cloud slid across the sun and the wind suddenly roughened, a gust of it slamming sound through the trees, flapping Cindy's skirt like the crack of a rifle. There was a smell of dust in the startled air.

Something in Craftner's expression subtly altered. "Mebbe you better give me the rest of it."

"The rest of it," Cindy said calmly, "is that you've been here a year pulling down top pay and nothing about this situation has mended. You may have done what you could but it isn't enough. We'll see what Three Sixes can do with a new boss."

"So that's it!" Craftner's laugh was short. "I been halfway lookin' for something like this."

He took a half turn away, wheeling back with his cheeks gone a ruddier color. "I know what's junin' through your head. You got the same bastard itch your ol' man had! An' when you seen I wouldn't go along with your notions—"

"Who are you trying to fool with that talk?"

Craftner's down-flailing fist flung her words aside. "I had you pegged when you fetched in that bleach-eyed gunfighter Murgatroyd and built him into a straw boss under me. But he was too cold a stick for your purpose. You was afraid you couldn't keep him in line so now you've snaked in this new guy, Stroud. You ain't pullin' no wool over my eyes, Missy!"

To her left, a few steps back of her, one of the porch boards skreaked and the significance of this ground Cindy's cheeks a little finer. "Are you finished?"

"No, I ain't finished—an' I ain't about to be finished." A sudden rage seized Craftner and came out of his eyes in a malevolent glitter. "Your ol' man hired me to run this spread an' I aim to keep on runnin' it whether it suits your notions or not! This is too good a ranch—"

"Yes. A lot too good to be sold up the river to a man like Wafer. You've given your last order here. Mike Stroud will boss Three Sixes. You can work under him or you can draw your time."

"We'll see about that! I guess your father—"

"You can probably talk him around," Cindy nodded, "but it will do you no good. My father doesn't own this ranch any more. He has deeded it to me and I have made Stroud boss. If you have any complaints you can take them to Stroud.''

She turned away from him then to see Beulah May and Talbot Lee standing frozen on the gallery with their mouths open, staring. She stepped past them without speaking and went into the house.

STROUD was at the corrals throwing gear on his horse when a hand clamped roughly down on his shoulder.

He stared into the blazing eyes of the range boss. The man's dark cheeks were twisted with fury and there was a lot of that fury still bottled inside him.

Cold warning played over Stroud's spine like a draft. ''When you want my attention the call of my name will usually provide it. Now what's on your mind?''

''You're about to find out. Go pick up your roll.''

Stroud thought about that. There was something here which he could not quite fathom. A wildness drifted out of the man that was as easily felt as the low ground breeze rolling down off the mountains; and it turned Stroud still while his mind quested spookily over his backtrail.

''My roll's doin' fine where it's at,'' he said, and watched Craftner closely. There was something implacable in the way the man stood in that tree-filtered sunlight with his left side presented, booted feet wide apart.

Stroud suspected something then which had not occurred to him before. This Craftner was a gun-fighter, and he was profoundly astonished he had not guessed this sooner. Something additional then clicked over in his mind, the remembrance of this man holding talk last night in the shadows with the Stirrup boss. He understood then why the Three Sixes trail herds never got through.

He let out a slow breath. "You feelin' right certain this is in your best interests?"

"I'll take care of my interests. You're gettin' off this place. Get your stuff an' start hikin'."

"You better look again at your hole card. I've no intention of leavin' Three Sixes."

The fingers of Craftner's right hand crooked and spread. His voice came out in a dry rustle of sound. "You want it the hard way? By God, you can have—"

"I'm askin' you, Craftner, do you reckon Wafer's payin' you enough to get killed for?"

Stroud's words hit the range boss with all the impact of bullets. A startled look fanned out of his jerked-open eyes and his twisted cheeks showed an angry confusion.

"I guess," Stroud said, "you're so used to your stink you figure no one else can whiff polecat around here. You must feel right proud of yourself, takin' pay for helping her while you steal a girl blind."

Craftner choked out a curse and slammed the hand at his gun butt.

"Go ahead—drag it!" Stroud threw at him mockingly. "Let's see how big a wolf you got."

In the frozen quiet Craftner stood tangled in his own mixed emotions. The suddenness of Stroud's reversal, that ringing challenge, the cold mockery of his look, shocked the Three Sixes boss into complete immobility.

"Well," Stroud said, "what are you waitin' for?"

Had this outlander talked that way five minutes ago Craftner would have killed him. Certainly he'd have tried. Now he stood in the grip of some strange paralysis. Short seconds ago he had been hotly filled with the lust to murder. That lust was still in him but its heat was gone, dissipated and scattered to the four winds by doubt.

"Got a cramp in your trigger finger?" Stroud's smile was taunting.

An impotent rage boiled through Link Craftner yet he did not dare lift the gun from his holster for he was convinced that if he did it would be the last act of a life he was far from ready to relinquish.

He let his hand fall away. "You've got me wrong—"

Stroud's smile merely broadened. "Only thing I can't put my finger on is what fetched you out in the open like this. Was it *me* Wafer was talkin' to you about last night? Did he tell you to run me off this spread?"

"You're loco!" Craftner blustered. "If you seen him talkin' to someone last night it sure wasn't *me!* I been fightin' that feller tooth an' toenail. Hell, you *couldn't* of seen him talkin' to me. I never went near town—"

"Who said anything about town? How'd you know it was in town I saw you?"

"I—why . . . Where else would I be likely to see Dan Wafer?" Craftner did his best to pull himself together, cursing the mockery he saw in Stroud's stare, the scorn and contempt he read there.

"You never seen *me*. I was expectin' trouble last night from Stirrup. With a dance on in town an' probably half the range goin', it looked like a pretty fair chance they would visit us. I posted Dreen in the yard an' put the rest out with rifles. To make certain doubly sure, I spent most of the night ridin' round the south range.''

"You did, eh?''

In some queer way Stroud's smile had altered. Craftner, watching him, did not like it. Sweat showed its shine on the slants of his cheeks and he backed off a step, his widening eyes growing darker.

He cried desperately: "Don't look at me that way! Only reason I jumped you was account of Miz Cindy—''

"This had better be true.''

"It *is* true, damn you! She called me over just now an' said she owned this spread an' was makin' you boss.''

"Reckon that lets you out.'' Stroud's grin changed again. "There's no room at my wagon for a bushwhacker's blankets.''

With all his muscles loosened Craftner stared at him stupidly.

Still with that thin, mocking smile on his mouth Stroud let Link Craftner see where he stood. "Always been told the Thief River was snake country. There's big snakes an' little snakes but only one kind that don't give out a warnin'. The kind that put Curly to ridin' the south fence. I'm wonderin' if it wasn't that same wrigglin' varmint that sunk his yellow fangs into Curly's back.''

Craftner's eyes showed fright. He flung a wild and frantic glance across the planes of Stroud's face. His sagging cheeks turned the color of wet chalk and he cried out in a wholly scared voice: "I never done it! I swear to God I never touched him!''

"Then what the hell are your knees shakin' for?''

Craftner's mouth worked like the jaws of a fish.

"Accordin' to the crew," Stroud said inexorably, "it was you told Curly to ride that fence; an' it was you told me, when you denied bein' in town, that you spent the whole night rammin' round the south range. You're a liar and a cheat and a dirty sneakin' dog—do I have to say more?"

Craftner's eyes were enormous. "I swear to God I never done it!"

With a snort of disgust Stroud turned on his heel.

Cheeks hideously bloated, his dilated eyes gone the color of murder, Craftner's hand flew down and caught hold of his iron.

Too late he realized that Stroud was still turning, that he had not started off but had swung completely around. Too late Craftner saw the dark gleam of leveled pistol, the coldly malicious curve of Stroud's smile.

His own gun was still clearing leather when flame burst whitely from the barrel of Stroud's.

8

THE LOBO GROWLS

A PASSIONATE hatred of Stirrup's conniving boss was beginning to occupy an unwonted amount of Stroud's attention. It had begun last night when Wafer had accosted him in that store at Thief River, offering him work after observing Cindy's interest. Many things during the interim had added fresh fuel, and what had just happened between himself and Cindy's range boss had done little to reduce the sultry heat of his convictions.

When Stroud had told Lee's daughter he would not step into Craftner's boots he had had his own reasons and those reasons still were valid. He did not blame Cindy for wanting to be rid of a man she couldn't trust. That was all right. She had given Stroud plain warning she would use every means she could find to save Three Sixes, and that was all right, too. He could even admire her singleness of purpose. But this unconcerned willingness deliberately to gamble with the lives of other people was not a quality he liked to find in a woman.

He was halfway to the house when she stepped through the gallery door, stopping as she caught sight of him. He would have given more than a little then to have been able to read her expression, to know if she'd been worried, but he was still too far away. All he could tell for sure was that he was suddenly impelled to hurry; and he didn't like that, either.

She had the reddest lips, the whitest teeth and the greenest eyes he had ever encountered—and the most aggravating composure, he told himself bitterly when he was near enough to see it. He knew damned well it was that shot had pulled her out here but no one would ever guess it if he were to judge by the look of her face. Any woman but her would have been plumb bug-eyed with questions but all she had to say to him was, "Do you find Beulah May more of a lady than I am?"

He felt heat pouring into his cheeks but he left the hat where it was on his head and took enough time to control his temper. "I came over here," he said, "to report a shootin'."

"I thought Murgatroyd—"

"I'm talkin' about Link Craftner. You worked that deal slick and it panned out just as you figured it would, except that Craftner ain't dead. I only busted his gun hand."

"You must have been pretty sure of yourself to have taken a risk like that," Cindy said. "What are you going to do with him?"

"The point," Stroud said, "is what are you going to do for a ramrod?"

She met his dark stare with a cool regard. "My offer to you is still open—"

"I thought so. Don't you ever get tired of makin' tracks like a man?"

He liked the color that came into her face. It reminded him of the girl he had met in Thief River and showed that much of her composure, like the rapier sharpness of her mind and decisions, was something which, out of sheer desperation, she'd been forced to acquire.

"Oh, Mike," she cried—"if you only knew!" Then her face was buried against his shoulder and his arms were around her and her body was shaking against his body; and his anger against Dan Wafer grew.

He lost track of time. It was the sound of a traveling horse brought his head up and Cindy, feeling him stiffen, pulled herself out of his arms.

She turned away from him, wiping her cheeks. "They'd just told me," she said, and stood a moment slack-shouldered. "Dad died half an hour ago—Beulah May found him. It was his heart, I guess . . . all that whisky."

She came around, trying to straighten her face out, and sent a dull glance in the direction of the road. "There's no one left now but Loosh. Loosh and me." She spoke as though all the courage were drained out of her. "What are we going to do, Mike?"

Stroud was watching the approaching rider, narrowly studying the horse, the way the man sat his saddle. It was no one he knew.

He said, answering her question, "You've got to hit back."

"But how can I?"

"Get yourself a good man—"

"I think," Cindy said, "I've got a good man," and she was looking straight into his eyes when she said it.

It was Stroud who finally had to tear his look away. "All right," he said gruffly. "I'll rod this fight on the strict understandin' I'm to be the boss, all the way, every minute an' without let or hindrance. You hirin' me like that?''

''Can you save Three Sixes?''

''I can try,'' Stroud said; and then the rider came up and, leaning from the saddle, handed Cindy a note. He was a thin, cold-jawed, hard-twisted little man who, when he'd done his chore, touched his hat and rode off.

Cindy tore open the note. Her eyes went through it quickly and then, darkening, again. She stood a long while staring into the distance while the run of time tramped across Stroud's nerves and the look of her turned him tighter and tighter.

At last she let out a ragged breath and, without turning, reached the note to him blindly.

Have incontrovertible proof and will expose your brother as man behind stealing of Three Sixes cattle unless Stroud agrees to leave country at once.

9

INVASION

"THAT'LL be Wafer, I reckon." Stroud, speaking out of a long silence, savagely crumpled the note in his fist and was about to hurl it wrathfully from him when some newer thought made him thrust the thing in his pocket. "He doesn't give you much choice."

Cindy, staring into the faroff yonder, seemed lost in the play of the wind-tossed shadows bluely rolling across the range from where, in the south, a storm was building, the clouds in that quarter towering dark and ominous.

A reflection of that darkness lay across the girl's features, deepening and shifting with the pulse of her thoughts. He read anguish into the slant of her eyes. Despair had given them the opaqueness of jade; and a hot, prodded anger prowled through Stroud's arteries.

He understood well enough what was in the girl's mind. Love of the soil was in her blood. Every acre of this ranch had for her its own cherished memories, its significance. She stood trapped between two courses, either of which must seem hatefully unfair. How could any girl throw her brother to the wolves! Yet how could

Cindy, with her intense and passionate feeling about Three Sixes, bring herself to send away the only man she had found who appeared to stand any chance of being able to save it?

She said without turning, "What could they do to Loosh?"

"I don't know. Do you reckon there could be any truth in this charge?"

She seemed to think about that, saying finally, "Loosh sets a lot of store on appearances. He likes to be around people and in some ways, I guess, he could be easily led. He likes to play cards and Dad has always regarded cards as one of the devil's worst inventions. He gave Loosh an allowance of two dollars a month—"

"Didn't pay him wages?"

"You'd have to know my father to understand that. He had his own way of looking at things. A strong believer in divine guidance, he thought of himself as a good provider, a better than average husband, a proper father and a man who was just in all his dealings. Conscience never nagged him for his treatment of the Wafers; he considered that a despoiling of the Philistines. But everyone didn't look at things his way. He saw no point, for instance, in wasting good money on fripperies for Mother. He believed togging his daughter out in pretty dresses the same as heading her straight for perdition. He felt that a man who would one day come into a good thing should be willing to work for it on that expectation."

"He doesn't sound like the kind who would look on himself as his brother's keeper."

"Uncle Tal?" She smiled faintly. "You can't blame Tal for trying. He's an awfully good talker."

"Do you know if he got around to putting up his pitch?"

Cindy said, "Mike, it's Loosh I'm worried about. What am I going to do?"

"You askin' me or handin' me the problem?"

Cindy met his eyes straightly. "Do you really think I'd let Dan Wafer parade my brother to this country as a thief?"

"You let your Dad deed this ranch to you, didn't you?"

"He wasn't the man to be influenced by a woman."

"I didn't say you influenced him. But he gave you the ranch—"

"He gave Three Sixes to me because he figured Dan Wafer would do Loosh out of it."

"Then we'll regard this note as a bluff. Wafer's made up his mind he doesn't want me around. He doesn't know your father's dead. He figures to use a little pressure and see if it won't scare him—"

"Wafer knows Dad better than that."

"You mean he wouldn't bluff?"

"Cyrano Lee would say, 'If Loosh has been stealing he will have to take his medicine.' "

"Then," Stroud said, "he meant the note for you."

Cindy nodded.

Stroud considered the angles. "Where is Loosh now?"

Her expression changed, or perhaps it only seemed to change because the shadows in her cheeks got deeper. The gleam of white teeth came through her red lips and she said without inflection, "Who can tell where a tomcat goes or where it will be ten minutes from now?"

Stroud took his eyes off her. He said bleakly, "It could still be a bluff, but we'd better not bank on that. If he's actually got some proof and he's made a deal with Redcliff—"

"Ben won't operate out here."

"He wouldn't need to. If Loosh shows up in town—"

"But wouldn't my father have to press charges?"

"If they hoped to make it stick. They wouldn't care about that. He aims to use this as a bluff to cut you loose of me. Then he'll show his spots and use it again to tar Three Sixes with the accusation you flung at him. Don't forget you've called him a cow thief—"

"Don't you think he is?"

"I'm not sure yet. But he will use whatever it is he's got to convince the rest of this country it's the Lees who are on the rustle. We can't afford to let him put Loosh in jail."

"If I know anything of the way he works he'll have Loosh in his hands or in hiding right now, waiting to see which direction I jump."

"I reckon that's pretty straight thinkin'," Stroud said. "There ain't none of this going to be at all easy. I expect I'd better mosey around; we've got to find something we can get our teeth in. I'll talk with Craftner. Meanwhile you can tell the crew they've got a new boss and put them to roundin' up beef for a trail herd. We can't fool around with that note coming due."

His remarks made sense, but he knew he was only talking now, trying to throw up a wall with a string of words; and he waited for her words to topple it over and, when she didn't speak, his head turned quickly to find her watching him.

Something dark and troubled came through her expression and he knew it had nothing to do with Loosh or Dan Wafer or the club Stirrup's boss held over her.

The feeling he had tried to wall up with words was out in the open, palpitating between them, too strong and too recognized by each of them to be longer shut away and ignored. The muscles worked in her throat and he knew he was fighting a losing battle, knew his treacherous feet were taking him toward her. He had never known eyes could be so green. Dark and still and troubled as they had been, they were now widely open, luminous and glowing like banked coals in the draft of an unlatched door.

Her breath was coming slow and so deep it tightened the shirt across her breasts; and he felt again the full unsettling effect of her, the more frightening because of its demonstrated power to make him ignore things he could not forget.

He was like a man dying of thirst beside a pool of clear water, afraid to put out a hand lest he shatter the sweet enchantment of life's last illusion.

He pulled his shoulders together.

"Well—I'm off," he said gruffly, but did not turn away.

Cindy's still shape stayed in its tracks also, and suddenly she was smiling in a way that cut asunder the last frayed stayropes of his logic. He knew with a terrible clarity there could be no permanence or future to their relationship, that this unswervable impulse was the call of flesh to flesh, a fundamental urge, a wanton surrender of principles to hunger.

He felt the trembling of her hand but she was not Lucinda Lee nor he Mike Stroud any longer. They were just two lonely people caught in the toils of something stronger than themselves. Her head went back, passion breaking through the pride which normally shaped her features, and his own stubborn head was bending to meet the unfolding petals of half-parted lips when the gallery's screen door skreaked on its hinges.

"Oh! I'm sorry," Beulah May's throaty tones said composedly.

Stroud stepped back with his cheeks hot as fire.

Cindy's green eyes darkened. But the face she turned toward the girl on the gallery was as coolly controlled as Beulah May's own.

"Mike has just agreed to be our new range boss—"

"I'm sure he'll be very efficient."

Stroud, feeling hotter, swore under his breath. The situation was not improved when the conviction got hold of him that Cindy's patrician cousin had discerned his embarrassment and was enjoying it.

Dark of face he said, "I'll be gettin' on," and bolted.

CRAFTNER was not in the bunkhouse when Stroud stepped inside. And the bedding was gone from the corner bunk.

Not yet sure of what this meant but suspecting, Stroud went to the far window and thrust his head out. Craftner's tracks were plain on the ground underneath. He'd been moving careful and had not gone for his horse because from where he stood now Stroud could see the blaze-faced bay swishing flies in a corner of the nearest corral.

Stroud picked up his rifle and went out through the window. Craftner's sign angled off toward the rear of the harness shed and there was a pretty good chance he might be over there somewhere lying in wait. It would be his style, Stroud decided; but he wasn't in the harness shed nor anyplace about it.

Not yet convinced he wasn't still on the place, Stroud went carefully through the rest of the outbuildings before, genuinely puzzled now, he went back to the bunkhouse. He found Craftner's bedroll spread out on the top bunk farthest removed from its former location. There was dried blood from his wounded hand on the tarp and one of his blankets had a piece torn out of it from which the man had probably fashioned a bandage.

It began to look like Craftner had hauled his freight, but it was uncommon odd that he had set off afoot. That Craftner hadn't cared to exchange any further words with him was entirely understandable, but not to the point where he would set off afoot rather than chance Stroud's attention by going for his horse. Town was a long eight miles from this place.

Possibly Craftner wasn't aiming for town. If he was in Wafer's pay, as Stroud strongly suspected, he might not need a horse to get where he was going. He would probably hit for Stirrup's closest boundary. That would be the Boxed Circle, north and east of Three Sixes.

Stroud wished he were better acquainted with this country. A little more knowledge as to the location of the various roundabout ranches and the distances between them could be a very useful thing he decided. And the swiftest way of acquiring it would be to circulate around.

So minded, he went over to the cook shack and told Go Slow to put him up enough grub for a two-day trip. Thinking ahead of the game now, he returned to the bunkhouse and took his bed apart, leaving on the bunk all spare clothing, miscellaneous belongings and one of his blankets. Shouldering the reconstructed bedroll he went over to the corrals and roped him out a tough looking baldfaced grulla which seemed snorty enough to have a lot of miles left unused inside him. But as he was about to lead the grulla out Stroud changed his mind and flipped his rope off. If he wanted to give a show of riding out of this country the impression might be more readily absorbed if he were seen on the horse which had fetched him into it. With this thought in mind he put his saddle on the gaunted roan, lashed his bedroll behind it, thrust his rifle in the boot and picked up the rations the halfbreed cook had fixed him. Riding back to the bunkhouse window he took up the trail of the departed ex-foreman.

CRAFTNER'S sign, when he got straightened around, led directly east. It went through the brush on a kind of rabbit run, angling upslope through manzanita and Spanish dagger interspersed now and again with dwarf cedar and taller, heavier growth. Craftner, by his tracks, was proceeding cautiously and taking a deal more time to the job than a man would think he'd care to if his object, as Stroud suspected, was to avoid any further meetings with the man who had smashed his gun hand.

On the crown of the hill the trail ducked into a stand of second growth pine and Craftner's pace perceptibly quickened. With this screen of trees between himself and pursuit the departing Three Sixes ramrod had thrust out his neck and started heating his axles in grim earnest. He wasn't running, of course, but he wasn't picking wildflowers, either.

Stroud was not too sure he could get anything out of him if he did catch up with Craftner. He was going along mostly just for the ride and because he wanted to know the man's destination. Too, it seemed to Stroud the man must have some exceptionally good and thus far unsuspected reason for taking such a Spartan means of departure. That busted hand must be giving him hell.

There were a number of things about this deal that Stroud couldn't quite get set in his mind. He didn't like, for instance, the way Talbot Lee had turned up again after staying away from the ranch all these years. It seemed a little too pat, a little too much like a gathering of the vultures, to suit Mike Stroud. There was nothing unnatural about Tal Lee coming back, but it was odd just the same; and then Cindy's father dropping dead like that, and being found that way by the returned man's daughter.

But if this Lee were an imposter, what in the devil was his game? Wafer wouldn't need two spies on the place. And it was preposterous to think he'd come all the way from Tonopah that his supposed relationship would be good for a touch. If he had the part down that well he would have known any loan he might get from Old Man Lee wouldn't be worth half the bother he'd have to go to to get it. Any impersonation good enough to make the grade would have to be set up on a firsthand knowledge of the subject and on the subject's terms of intimacy with Cindy's father. The Talbot Lee who had arrived appeared to have that knowledge, for hadn't Cindy said they'd talked of the old times here, of favorite horses and stuff like that?

Just the same, Stroud didn't like it. He couldn't make himself like it and he was firmly convinced they were not through with Redcliff. Any galoot who'd spend his money to keep old Lee drunk—and so continuously fuddled as to set up a heart condition—wasn't shooting for marbles or going to pull for the tules just because the odds were suddenly shifted round a little.

Something else that bothered Stroud was that outstanding note that would fall due in sixty days. It didn't make any difference whether the commission house which held it would renew the terms or not; that note represented real menace. And Craftner knew about it.

Did he also know who held it?

One thing was certain: the quicker Three Sixes marketed some beef the better Stroud would feel about the entire business. It wouldn't change his feelings about Cindy but it might ease up some of the pressure that was riding him, some of the conflict in loyalties which was making this job hell.

A low mutter of sound rolled out of the south and a stronger gust of dampened wind fluttered the wipe at Stroud's bronzed neck and set his vest points flapping. The ground climbed steadily upward and this was become a pretty rough country with the second growth pine given over hereabouts to incense cedar and bigcone spruce with a very thin sprinkling of Douglas fir. Twisting round in the saddle for a look across his shoulder, Stroud saw the clouds massed high and black in the direction of Thief River and, even as he looked, lightning ripped twice across them and thunder shook its deep rumble through the roundabout hills.

He was turning back when he stopped with stiffened muscles, his attention riveted on a place far below and possibly fifteen miles as the crow flies to the southeast of his present placement. There was a long grayish

patch on the dun terrain there which an unversed East-
erner would probably have taken for a lake, but Stroud
did not. He recognized its significance even before,
through continued watching, he discerned its steady
progression.

So large a body of water in that neighborhood would
have been priceless; what Stroud actually saw, spread
like a dirty gray blanket over range held sacred to cattle
since the first white settlers had wrested it from the
Apaches, was a blight which might well drive the
ranchers of this region to the very brink of madness.
Sheep—the curse of all cowmen. Thousands of them,
mowing down the graze like locusts.

Even here with the naked eye Stroud could follow
their track back across the range clear to the slot where
it passed through the blue horizon, a dun desolation left
behind their sharp black hooves.

A sight to arrest any cowman's glance, it made
Stroud's shine like polished agate. There could be no
doubt of their intention. They were headed straight for
Three Sixes!

10

CAUGHT FLAT FOOTED

A HUNDRED wild thoughts might have flown through
Stroud's head as he stood in the stirrups looking down
on that scene. Actually he was stunned, far too jammed
with emotion to think very clearly about anything.

Sheep!

It seemed incredible that his malign fate should have
brought sheep into this country just now. But wasn't it
equally incredible to believe Wafer back of this? Sheep
were no respecters of boundaries. They denuded the
range and polluted its streams with malignant venom
which took no accounting of ownership. No self-
respecting cow would eat or drink after them; and
Wafer was a cattleman, knowing all this.

No matter who was behind them these sheep spelled
trouble—bad trouble. A lot of this country was still
good range but if the sheep came in here two years from
this date it would be crisscrossed with gullies and inside
of five years it would be nothing but badlands, gutted
and useless. There never had been a sheep and cattle
war anywhere that left anything but blackest ruin in its
wake. Look at Pleasant Valley!

He was minded, when some of the red fog lifted, to whirl the gaunt roan forthwith and ride down there. But, precious as he knew time to be in this deal, he understood with a bitter thoroughness that you could not go off half cocked with a sheepman and expect to come up with the long end of the stick.

Sheep had become a big business; there was no use fooling yourself about that. The days of the gentle-eyed shepherds were finished. The present handlers of sheep were a merciless breed who had learned their grim lesson in the school of hard knocks and they knew every trick in the deck. Cowmen hadn't learned anything and during the last few years, in every battle over grass, the sheep had come out winners by such margins it was ludicrous—and don't think the sheepmen weren't laughing about it!

Cowmen couldn't get it through their heads that times had changed. They were still placing their faith in the efficacy of systems as outmoded as tin pants, being too bull-headed to catch significance in current happenings. As a last resort they always fell back on gunplay—their inevitable answer to every major problem—and those who weren't left for the buzzards to chew on generally wound up in jail or on the end of a rope. The way to beat sheep was to use the guns first and never let the bastards get a toe-hold. You might still wind up behind bars or on the owl-hoot, but your family, at least, would still have a ranch worth working. If you were lucky, that is.

Stroud's face, as his mind played over these things, was blacker than the clouds piling up in the south; but he had learned quite a bit during these past few months. He had learned with extreme reluctance to bow to the inevitable. Facts were facts and sheep was big business showing much greater profits than could be taken out of cattle. Maybe Dan Wafer *was* back of this, maybe his vision was more acute than he got credit for and the stakes he was playing for larger than those apparent. If he could turn this whole vast country into sheep he might ruin the range but he would pile up more wealth than was behind a lot of kingdoms—and why the hell should he care what happened to the range? With all that money he could live where he pleased.

These sheep could not be ignored or long left alone but, as Stroud, now thinking carefully, saw it, the need here and now was for first things first. Those woollies had a long way to come yet. They were apparently following the course of the river and were still some four or five miles east of town. Probably skirting the community they would creep on up the river another four or five miles before leaving it to spill out across Three Sixes' lower pastures. They would not make many miles in a day; therefore one more night's leeway would not fetch them sufficiently close to make a stand impracticable. In the meantime there was Craftner, and Stroud wanted very much to know where Craftner was going.

The man was getting artful, crossing bare rock each time he got the chance now, doing his best to confuse any possible pursuit by leaving hard surface in all manner of directions. Stroud, with Craftner's trend pretty well in mind by this time, ignored these excursions and continued bearing east.

Though he kept his eyes alert to scan each covert for possible ambush, his mind stayed with the sheep. Most of the larger sheep kings now were organized in a tough and obstreperous association which was quick to act in behalf of its members. They had made it tough on cowmen who came out to meet sheep at gunpoint. In one of the cases Stroud knew about where a cowman had killed a herder, all the circumstances proved self-defense but the cowman was hanged for it, anyway. Stroud knew this for "pressure," which it was, the sheep crowd controlling the courts in that country; but a lot of big cowmen had pulled in their horns and had since been sheeped out of the business.

You just couldn't give a damned sheepman a thing. For every mile you gave up they would grin and take ten. There was only one way to deal with their kind and, if he could get the backing of some of these ranchers, he believed he could guarantee to keep the sheep out. It might entail a hereafter, but what a man got for nothing was seldom worth more. Tomorrow, while there was time, he'd put his cards on the table.

He must, he knew, be getting close to Craftner. He'd come pretty near four miles and it seemed hardly in the cards to assume the man had got much farther. A full hour had passed since Stroud had ridden from the yard and, even granting the man a twenty minute start, he was not at all likely with his wound to have done much better.

Stroud stopped the roan for a backward look. It was entirely possible he had overridden the man and that Craftner, instead of ahead of him, had not actually come this far. He commenced casting around for tracks again and abruptly found them. By all the signs and signal smokes they were not much over five minutes old.

Less thought and more vigilance seemed indicated.

He did not want Craftner to spot him first; he didn't want Craftner to discover him at all.

He swung out of the saddle and tied the reins to a tree. The trees were getting thinner here, the growth running more to brush and saguaro cactus. It was doubtful if Craftner intended going much farther; in high-heeled boots and with a gunshot paw he had gone just about as far as he'd be able. Following his tracks Stroud pushed forward, Indian quiet and Indian careful.

Seen across the arm of a giant cactus and through a scattering of runted spruce the terrain before him saucered out to shape a rosebowl basin whose height of land, short yards ahead, was crossed by posts and strands of wire. This, Stroud judged, would be a boundary. He looked about with sharpened eyes.

Groundslope formed a natural trail here with the fugitive's sign, increasingly distinct, telling its tale of panicked haste. Craftner, dropping into this pocket, had lifted his pace to a shambling run. He had, very obviously, caught sight of Stroud.

A few cows marked with the iron of Boxed Circle watched Stroud suspiciously before at last resuming their interrupted lunch. Stroud's eyes, narrowed now with a flinty brightness, followed the trail across the hollow, climbing with it up the opposite slope to where it disappeared in a stand of brush. His glance stopped there while he considered its possibilities. Not liking them, he retraced his steps to where he'd left the roan, untied its reins and climbed into the saddle. Swinging wide to the right he set off with the intention of circling the basin.

But after five hundred yards of cautious travel a new

thought swung him left again, pulling him up in a thicket of spruce for another look into the saucer's depression. The browsing cattle raised their heads again and a sharper thought clicked over in Stroud's mind. It would be a pretty smart stunt to use cows for a lookout.

Even as the thought cut through his head something slammed past his face and the crack of a rifle came out of that brush, its clatterous echoes banging off the slopes. Stroud raked the gelding's flanks with his spurs and low on its neck whipped through the spruce, dragging his saddle gun out of its scabbard.

He went three hundred yards and stopped, setting the roan suddenly back on its haunches, but no rumor of sound drifted to him; and he put the gelding back into motion, letting him pick his way at his own easy walk in the bend of the circle he had so recently abandoned.

"Playin' slick," he thought, with his mind on Craftner. "Makin' out to stampede, then layin' back there in that brush like a bobcat."

To the left just ahead there was a roll of higher ground with the fluted columns of three tall saguaros lifting out of it like feathers from the scalp of a painted brave. He judged it would overlook the pocket but he did not make the mistake of appearing there. Instead, swinging right, he dropped back into the screen of spruce and again pointed east, whispering over the needled ground with nerves tight cocked and rifle ready.

A cleared place lay before him now with nothing coming out of the burnt adobe but the purplish pads of prickly pear growing in clumps to the height of a man's belt. Moreover the five-strand fence of barbed wire crossed it presenting him with its own brand of problem.

He could not jump that barrier on horseback nor could he take the gelding through without breaking it. That wire had been stretched by wagonwheel and was drawn so taut that if he attempted to cut it the news would fly like the blast of a trumpet. Craftner would be warned immediately; so, too, would any Boxed Circle hands who might happen to be in the vicinity. And Boxed Circle now was a part of Stirrup. Stirrup's hands would not be niggardly in extending hospitality if they came across Stroud the wrong side of that wire.

But even as he considered these facts Stroud was getting out of the saddle. He led the roan behind the nearest trees and, as these weren't strong enough to hold him, hobbled him there with his neckerchief. This done, he roved several quick glances over the view, got down and started a snail-like progress across the pear-studded open.

He had not realized it was so hot till he got down there with his chin in the dust and commenced his crablike haul for the wire.

All wind had died and, though the sun's bright disc was locked behind a veil of cloud, the air was like something drawn off a furnace. Sweat ran down his cheeks like rain; even the backs of his hands were beaded with it and he thought he could not crawl another step. But at last he found himself under the wire.

He lay there a moment, stretched flat and panting with his heart knocking heavily against his wet chest. And the hell of it was that he was not done yet. A lone spanish bayonet thrust its dagger points out of the ground twenty paces ahead at the edge of a halfhearted tangle of chaparral, and wisdom advised him to get beyond that. Not that he thought Link Craftner might see him but because if anyone else did they would shoot just as quick very probably and perhaps with much greater efficiency.

It would have been hard enough to have made this trip without baggage; to make it lugging a rifle was unadulterated torture. He had to drag his slingless repeater by the barrel, be alert against the chance of its glint being detected and watch out all the while not to bang it on a rock or stop it up with dirt. But he clung onto it doggedly, well knowing the shape he would be in if caught this side of the fence without it.

When he finally lifted himself onto his knees he could not see Craftner. Nor could he see him standing up. There was a sandstone ledge between himself and the pocket, and he wondered once again if this trek were worth the risk. Even if he came up behind Craftner and managed to get the drop there was no guarantee that he could make the fellow talk. All Stroud wanted was the answer to one question but it was all too apparently possible that Craftner might not have it.

He dragged off his hat and knocked the sweat from his forehead. Beyond the ledge a windfall blocked his direct advance. He would have to make another jog to the right to get past and, looking to see if he could, he found the hogback in that direction thickly grown to ragweed and nettle. These weeds, dead and dry now, might throw off a lot of sound if he should try to get through them.

It was just about time, he thought, to call it a day.

Craftner, on guard now, might expect him to try

some kind of flanking movement. He may have shifted his position. And if there were anyone else within a mile of this place they were bound to have heard the report of that shot. If Craftner were as crooked as Stroud suspected, he would have established some means of communication through Boxed Circle and some of their hands might be coming up now.

Stroud clapped on his hat and took a squint at the sky. It was still overcast though the storm in the south seemed to be blowing itself out. With his glance coming down again Stroud's shape went rigid.

This hogback which formed the pocket's east rim fell sharply away beyond the ragweed and nettles in a kind of gulch or ravine and what had caught at Stroud's interest was a section of roof with a stovepipe sticking out of it.

Off to the left of him he heard brush break and he turned half around to his right and started running, not toward the fence but parallel with it and away from the pocket. A gun went off somewhere back of him and another gun barked somewhat closer and to the left, and he caught the high whine of ricocheting lead. Scared, but more angered, he stuck to open ground where the sound of his travel would not so quickly betray him. He heard a garble of voices and Craftner's enraged shout tearing through them: "There he goes, damn him— Cut him down! Cut him down!"

All hell broke loose then with at least three rifles trying to knock the legs from under him; and he ducked into the line of spruce with lead spatting into dirt and wood all about him.

Turning sharply left he ran three strides and stopped short, muscles bunching. He let out a gusty breath, lips tightening cruelly. Bent double he sprinted on, hearing Craftner yell: "The wire, you fools! He's tryin' to get to his horse!"

Smiling thinly then Stroud dropped to lower ground, angling northeast behind the thinning line of trees. They could have the roan and welcome but if they wanted to nail his hide to the fence they were going to have to pay dearly for it. He had no doubt now where the butter on Craftner's bread was coming from.

Running out of the spruce he found himself less than a hundred yards to the south of and below the line shack the top of whose roof he had glimpsed through the ragweed. This was a Boxed Circle camp but the three saddled geldings standing on dropped reins and watching him inquiringly from the yonder confines of a pole corral showed Stirrup's iron burned into right cheeks.

He made straight for the corral, having no desire to play hide and seek through the brush with Stirrup gun wranglers. He had not found the answer to the question that was bothering him but he had learned everything he needed to know about the loyalty status of Cindy's former range boss. The sooner he got away from here the better he was going to like it.

Not wanting to alarm the horses any more than he could help, he slowed into a walk as he went up the slope. The corral was set against the east wall of the cabin and was big enough to hold possibly half a hundred steers, though none were now in it. The horses with cocked ears continued to eye him suspiciously but made no attempt to move out of their tracks, thus showing themselves to be broken and reliable.

Coming up to the gate, a look thrown across his shoulder failed to disclose any evidence that Craftner's friends had yet caught onto his ruse. He had the top bar out of its slot and was lifting the middle one when lead knocked it splintering out of his hands.

With a smothered curse he dived for the horses who, now panicked with the sound of unseen hornets, the vicious cracking of rifles and Stroud's own suddenly incautious approach, flung up their heads and with flying reins bolted to the pen's far side.

Dropping back of the bars, Stroud thrust his rifle through, noting the extent of his danger in one glance. Having found his horse without sign of himself someone, probably Craftner, had guessed his intention and, fetching the rest of them, had swung back to stop him.

They had a better than average chance of succeeding.

11

THE LONG GUNS BARK

THE three geldings were bunched explosively together
at the pen's far curve eighty feet from Stroud's trapped
placement beside the half cleared gate. He had no rope
nor any likelihood of getting one short of the saddles
that were on the horses' backs. He could only reach the
horses by fully exposing himself to Stirrup's rifles and
should these fail to cut him down the terrified animals,
the moment he started toward them, would almost
certainly bolt. They would not bolt toward him but
away from him and, in this circular pen, any chance he
had of catching one looked exceedingly remote. Before
he could hope to head them they'd be over the gate's
remaining rail and off with a burst of thundering hoofs.
He was too old a hand to try to fool himself now. When
those geldings got out of this pen he was done.

And the hell of it was this spot was not tenable. It
would be only a matter of time till one or another of
Craftner's friends made a lucky shot and picked him
off. Three peeled poles placed a foot apart, and with the
bottom one nearly two feet above ground, afforded
mighty thin cover against four men with rifles.

He was crouched behind the gate's left upright, a log fully thick enough to hold up a bridge. But this would serve only until Stirrup's gun hands sufficiently scattered to catch him between a crossfire. And they were already fanning out, firing only enough to keep him there while they scuttled and skittered into better positions, taking their time to it, satisfied in knowing time was on their side.

Stroud slammed another quick look at the geldings. If one of those slugs should happen to graze or come near them they would stampede just as surely as if he went after them. Sooner or later one of Craftner's amigos would catch hold of that thought and unlimber his rifle.

Still holding his fire Stroud scanned the surrounding terrain in the hope of being able to cut down the odds. But Craftner's crowd wasn't taking any chances. They had him sewed up and meant to keep him that way. One of their number was in the spruce but he was not exposing himself to Stroud's rifle. Another was up in those ragweeds someplace and a third, possibly Craftner, was working around behind the shack. The fourth man Stroud couldn't place, and it worried him. The east slope of this ravine held the highest ground round here and if one of Stirrup's hands could get into the brush that grew along its summit he could wrap this job up in about two minutes. It was a leadpipe cinch that was where the guy was bound for.

But Stroud couldn't spot him.

And time was running out.

He twisted his head for another look at the horses and a blue whistler jerked the brim of his hat. Another, from the ragweeds, tore a hole through its crown and knocked it slanchways across the left side of Stroud's head. One of the geldings reared up then with a terrible scream and Stroud, turned desperate by the knowledge that with these horses must go his last hope, rolled over and, closing his ears to the racketing rifles, brought his own gun up with a frantic prayer.

It was tricky business with the two geldings coming head on. He could see the wild roll of their terrified eyes, the laid-back ears, the distended nostrils. A madman's gamble; but he had heard wild horse hunters sometimes "creased" them and what they could do he could certainly try. He understood the trick was to fire in such manner the bullet grazed only those cords at the top of the neck just in front of the withers and close to the spinal column. A good deal of luck had to be taken for granted and even then the performance was not often successful—but he was at his last ditch. He couldn't catch these crazed horses barehanded and he sure couldn't get out of this deal on foot—not with four blazing rifles leveled at him.

He held his fire to the last possible moment. He felt inclined toward the sorrel with the flax mane and tail but the gray was the nearest and it was the gray he finally squeezed trigger on. For eight or ten instants hand-running nothing happened and he was persuading himself he had chalked up a miss when the gray went down in a tangle of legs. The sorrel spun on hind hoofs and fled squealing, but at the pen's far side the blood hotly pumping from the first downed horse set him crazy with fear and he came larruping back, eyes white-rimmed like a stallion bronc's.

One look at the gray's twisted crimson-stained neck told Stroud how far he'd get on that one, and with a bitter curse he whirled to the poles, driving three slugs at a blue-shirted sprinter who had jumped from concealment and was mowing down ragweed in a rush for the cabin. Stroud's second shot shook dust out of his vest and his third shot knocked the fight clean out of him and left him lying in a grotesque heap. Craftner's bullthroated roar sheered through the din with a berserk abandon: "Chop him down! Chop him down!"

The only chance Stroud had, as he saw it right then, was to someway manage to board the spooked sorrel that was rampaging toward him in mad drive for the gate. If he could only get his fingers on those flying reins—

The horse was ten paces off, and coming like an avalanche, when his left front hoof came down on a rein's end. The leather tore free but he was flung half around with his hauled-down head sharply jerked to left flank and his weight, off balance, careening heavily toward Stroud.

Doubling up on itself with the snap of a whiplash, the other rein ribboned past Stroud's turning face. With the swiftness of light his left hand snagged it while his spread right clawed for the bridled head.

Aching fingers desperately froze to the cheekstrap as the plunging beast went up on hind legs, Stroud swinging from his precarious hold like a pendulum, in and out between those flailing front feet, with the cold fear knotting the jerking muscles of his stomach while the animal's wild scream rang in his ears. If the horse thought to bite, those foam-flecked jaws could snap Stroud's defenseless arm like a matchstick. But he wouldn't let go. Not even the frenzied shaking of the crazed sorrel's head could dislodge his grip.

Stroud could feel the fetid pant of his breathing, and then a shod hoof raked white lightning across him and he thought for one agonized moment he couldn't possibly keep his fingers locked to that cheekstrap—but he did. With wave on wave of pain sweeping through him, his mind clung stubbornly to a vision of Cindy; knowledge of the overwhelming odds stacked against her steeling his determination, convulsively tightening the hold of slipping fingers.

Unable longer to support the pull of Stroud's weight, the gelding's head began reluctantly to sag. A kind of shudder ran through him and his forequarters dropped, his hoofs striking ground with a solid impact. He stood trembling, whickering timidly, while Stroud, half blinded by dust and sweat, sagged against his near shoulder, too used up to do more than hang there, numbed fingers still hooked in the twisted bridle.

A burst of rifle fire roused him to remembrance of Craftner, to the continuing menace of the original danger which had caused him to take such chances for this horse. He had gotten the horse and now he'd better get out of this. Whatever had temporarily silenced the guns, they were speaking again now with a redoubled fury.

The sorrel whimpered with fright and Stroud knew he had to pull himself out of this inertia and get aboard the horse and get the animal headed out of here if his aid were materially to increase Cindy's chances. He caught a handful of mane and the reins with his left while his right hand sought the cold brass of the horn and his lifted left boot tried to find the stirrup.

The sorrel snorted and took off the instant Stroud's weight settled into the oxbow, and it was all he could do

95

to get up into the saddle. His mind was clear now, fully aware of the danger, but his whole left side seemed to be stiffening up and he guessed that hoof had done more damage than he'd reckoned. He had no time to be worrying about it for all his thinking just now was taken up with the knowledge that somehow, someplace, he had lost his rifle.

The horse was building up speed, heating into full gallop with little snakeheads of dust beating up all about them, when he seemed of a sudden to hang fire in midstride. The beat of his reaching hoofs went off pace and anguish tore a thin scream from his throat. Stroud reckoned the end to be a matter of moments.

There was nothing more he could do to stave off the inevitable. The sun, burst free of its cumulus wrappings, was flooding the ravine with its bright furnace glare and a chilled sweat prickled the back of Stroud's neck. The wolves were out of their holes now, red tongues lolling between their bared fangs.

Tomorrow Stroud would have talked with the ranchers, only now there wouldn't be any tomorrow. There never had been any tomorrow for the man who had opened a cabin door and seen what there had been to see beyond it. Stroud understood this and had known from that moment the full truth about tomorrow. Tomorrow was nothing but a closed pine box with the name MIKE STROUD painted in black across the lid; a pine box waiting by a fresh-dug hole.

Stroud cursed the sheep and reached for his rifle, discovering once more that he no longer had it. It lay gleaming in the dust of the corral someplace, forgotten, abandoned when he'd leaped for this horse that was going to pieces between his knees. Already he could feel it wilting under him, all the drive fallen out of its sagging muscles, all the power of clean legs pouring out with the blood that was pumping bright red from the hole in its shoulder.

Stroud saw Craftner's shape with the sun winking back from his vest's silver buttons scrambling up the slope from the green line of spruce. He had a short-barreled belt gun in his left fist and a piece of dirty rag tied around his smashed right; the grin on his face was one of wicked enjoyment. There must be, Stroud thought, an enormous satisfaction in the man right now. He had the man who had replaced him just where he wanted him, flanked front and rear.

One back-thrown glance proved this to Stroud. The dying gelding had fetched him but a scant eighty yards from the pole corral. He had run upslope and was now on the ridge, an open target from every side with the slugs singing round him like angry hornets. The horse was reeling, floundering like a lost steer in a boghole, whimpering piteously.

When he felt the sorrel starting to fold Stroud kicked free of the oxbows and flung himself off. He struck the ground heavily but had the wit to keep rolling, making three revolutions before he got his legs under him and staggered erect. Lead shrilled from behind and whined before him as, pistol in hand and bent almost double, he broke into a lurching run for the ragweed.

It was the act of a man who had burned all his bridges. There was no percentage in such a fool move but it was better, Stroud thought, than making like a worm and trying to wriggle himself into some non-existent hole. Since there was nothing but death for him on this ridge he chose to meet death on his own brash terms, in the tradition of the service, not quailing like a coyote.

He had seen in that last backward look from the saddle that the Boxed Circle hand who had been back of that line shack had broken from cover and was now, with blazing rifle, coming up the ridge behind him. Craftner, coming up on his left, was still out of range, having nothing but a belt gun. There was no one on his right but the fence was too close and too exposed in that direction. The only chance, if there was one, would be to plow straight ahead toward the man in the ragweed. He could see him, just ahead, hunkered down on his bootheels, shoving fresh cartridges into his rifle.

Stroud was still too far off to make use of his pistol when he saw the black tube of that rifle come up, saw flame gout from the muzzle, saw dun earth rushing up at him. He thought, in that instant, of many things but it never occurred to him he had been hit. He knew he'd crashed into a gopher hole and it was this, he believed, which had thrown him.

He hardly noticed the shock of impact. All his faculties just then were pooled to the project of preserving his life and it was remarkable, he thought, how wonderfully agile such a purpose could make even a boneyard of mismatched cogs like his own. It had shown him, for instance, that the very shortest distance between two points was the way he was headed and that, to regain the horse he had left beyond the fence, he was going to have to do something about that pot-licking hound with the rifle up ahead, that grunt in the ragweeds, that Stirrup slug-slammer. And he was still of that opinion when he started to crawl forward.

He had to give it up. He couldn't quite figure what

the hell was the matter with him. He knew he could walk and he reckoned he could scuttle at a kind of a run once he got on his feet, but he sure wasn't going anywhere at a crawl. Every time he tried it someone hit him with a sledge and the place burned like fire when the rough ground pressed against it.

In a rash of cold sweat he finally got a knee under him and, after much trying, he managed to get off his elbows and crouch there swaying on a pair of braced hands. That was when he first noticed the widening stain on his shirt-front. It gave him quite a surprise to learn that some of Stirrup's lead hadn't been entirely wasted.

He reckoned he ought to tie it up. Feller in his condition couldn't spare all that blood—he hadn't hardly got over all he'd lost at that damn cabin.

Then he got to thinking, queerly, of something Douglas had said to him just before he'd pulled out of Nogales—he'd just got him that pair of big rowelled spurs with the fancy Mex danglers. "Yeah," Jeff Douglas had said dryly, "very lovely. But for chrissakes, Stroud, a guy on the dodge has to kind of use his head! Why'n't you take along the Fort Lowell band while you're at it?"

Stroud thought it was kind of funny, the idea of Douglas with those big silver spurs. All of life was kind of funny if you just stopped to think of it. He had sure been set up with those Mexican guthooks; forty-eight hard-earned bucks he had give for them and what the hell good were they doing him now? Out here on this ridgetop he would gladly have swapped those spurs and forty other things for the chance to get a leg across a live and willing horse.

But the only live horse around this patch of cactus was the one he had left tied down there beyond the wire. That was why he had to get himself up and keep going. You could die just as dead through the loss of blood as anything.

Those damn rifles were still talking. But all the bang and racket seemed to be coming from up in front of him and he thought that mighty queer because Craftner, even if he'd joined the guy up there in the ragweeds, didn't have nothing but a belt gun—or hadn't when Stroud last saw him And where in the devil was that guy from the line shack? Hell, it must be him! He must have joined that joker in the ragweeds; but how had he got past without Stroud seeing him and how come their slugs weren't beating the dust up?

He wondered if maybe he was getting delirious because, listening now, there didn't seem to be more than one rifle talking and the sound of its bark didn't seem to be coming from quite where it ought to—more from the west of his position, more in the direction of the fence than the way he had been headed, which was almost due south.

Stroud shook his head. Everything seemed to be getting jumbled up. He couldn't understand for one thing why, still hearing the vicious *crack crack* of that Winchester, he couldn't also hear the sibilant *whtt* of passing lead. That guy ought to take a few shooting lessons if he couldn't put his slugs any closer than that.

Now the feller had quit, was probably busy reloading. Now his pal back there on the ridge behind Stroud was tuning up again, proving he hadn't passed Stroud at all. Stroud reckoned he had just kind of imagined he had heard two guns in the weeds up ahead. That guy was still back of him but he was getting awful close.

And then a new thought pulled Stroud's lips back in a grin. Those two damn fools had got mixed up and were throwing all that hell's smear of lead at each other! Jeez—what a belly laugh! Each one of those bustards thought the other guy was Stroud!

But a new notion suddenly knocked all the laugh out of him. That vinegarroon behind him wasn't holed up like the other one, he was still on the prowl and getting closer while Stroud listened. Any moment now he might come worming into sight and . . .

Stroud reckoned he'd better be ready.

He got his other knee under him and twisted around with his butt sagging weakly back on his bootheels and sweat breaking out on him just like a dew. He didn't seem to have no more strength than a kitten and didn't even have enough peck to get mad about it. It took all his energy and all his concentration just to lift the damn pistol up onto his leg and, at that, he had to use both hands to keep it steady.

He was glad of one thing: he wouldn't have to wait long. Both those fellers had quit firing now and he could hear this nearest one rattling the weeds like a hydrophoby skunk moving through a field of corn shucks.

He wished to hell the guy would get a wiggle on.

Things were kind of blurring round the edges of his vision and he didn't know how much longer he could hold that frilling gun up. He never had known a forty-five to be so heavy.

He drew his muscles together and hooked a finger round the trigger.

He could see this sidewinder's track now and, even

as he looked, he saw another batch of weeds bend. A shock of rust-brown hair thrust into his vision with a touch of green back of it and, back of that, a faded shirt with sleeves rolled up around sunburnt forearms whose undersides, each time one came forward, showed a crisscrossed pattern of angry red weals where bits of brush had been ground into them.

He was inching along much as Stroud had awhile ago, belly down and pantslegs dragging, the most of his attention being more than taken up with the effort of keeping his smokepole free of dirt. He wasn't even bothering to lift his head up.

Stroud knew damn well he ought to shoot the dumb bastard and his mind told his hand to go ahead and do it, but the word didn't seem to get down to his finger. He had always thought shooting a gun pretty simple and not requiring enough sense to pound sand down a rat hole; yet here he was hunkered with a gun in both fists and not enough beans in the shotbox to use it.

Just about the time he was beginning to think this moleblind fool was going to crawl right on up into his lap, the gunman in the ragweeds let fly another slug. It whistled from the west and passed six feet behind the crawler, but the sound whipped him round and jerked him onto his haunches with the sun flinging light from that lifting barrel. Yet so anxious was this one to get his sights lined on that other rifle-packer that for one incredible hope-crammed moment his hate-narrowed glance missed Stroud entirely.

Stroud's mind tried to squeeze the trigger of his pistol but a fuse must have blown between brain cell and finger for no sound shattered the frozen quiet.

Something, then, pulled the man's head around.

Surprise exploded through the fellow's shocked stare. Recoil jarred him upright out of his crouch, fear rooting him there while his sweat beaded cheeks turned the color of panic.

Stroud watched his jammed thoughts congeal on the pistol. But when the piece failed to speak the whole bloated look of the man's blanched face altered.

The edge of a tongue flattened across his lips. Without warning he jumped two feet to the left, the barrel of his rifle whipping round to grim focus.

Stroud heard the crash and pitched down a long spiral into black oblivion.

12

SPUR SONG

STROUD had no idea how long he'd been out, but the sun had heeled far over. The first thing he saw when he got his eyes open was a section of clenched fist with a broken piece of ragweed loosely clutched between lax fingers.

The fist was in the yellow dust a couple of yards beyond Stroud's face and a head, half glimpsed behind it, showed a tousled mop of rust brown hair that idly swayed to each lift of breeze.

Stroud stared at that hair a long while without moving. He didn't have to see the guy's features or even that inch of green wipe that showed back of them. What he couldn't quite manage to get through his mind was why this galoot hadn't done a better job when he'd let go point blank with that rifle. Or why the damn fool was still forted up here.

Both answers were easy when, after another ten minutes, Stroud got himself up onto a knee and both elbows and, from this vantage, saw the back of the man's head.

One look was plenty.

He slumped back on the ground, knowing by the amount of sweat he'd brought out that he was in no shape for any prolonged effort. He could not understand why he should feel so damn weak. He'd been shot before, knocked down by experts, but he hadn't come to with any feeling like this. It was like he'd been dragged through a couple hundred knotholes. And he sure didn't like it.

But his mind was a lot less fuzzy now and he could tell by the shadows it was nearing four o'clock. Been out a lot longer than he'd imagined.

It was his thigh where that crazed sorrel's hoof had raked him that was giving him the most of his present uncomfort. A cursory inspection of his disheveled person failed to locate any damage that would put him to bed. Just a handful of nicks was the most those birds had given him. He had three or four places where near misses had burned him and one shallow bullet track across his left side. But all of these souvenirs had clotted and did not appear to have cost him any great amount of blood.

He reckoned mostly it was exhaustion which had whittled him down so and guessed he would feel more like himself once he'd got back into the harness for awhile.

At the cost of considerable grunts and exertion he finally got himself up onto his feet and, when he figured his stomach might stay where it belonged, he took another squint at the dead Stirrup gun wrangler.

The guy wouldn't drag down any ribbons for beauty. When he'd jumped to his feet and whipped around with that rifle, intending to settle Stroud's hash for him, someone had handed him a harp in short order. The slug must have struck him dead center between the eyes. It had gone right through and there wasn't much left where it had come out but hair and collar.

Stroud's muscles suddenly leaped and stiffened.

A long heavy shadow darkened the dust beside his own and, because it had not moved, he hadn't paid much attention to it. Not till he caught the restive stamp of a horse, the tinkle of spur chains, did the shape of that shadow assume significance. Only then did Stroud realize he didn't have his pistol, that it still lay in the dust where it had dropped from his hand.

Behind him a man's voice dryly said: "That feller ain't goin' no place. Turn around."

IT was very near dark when Link Craftner, on a lathered and just about pooped-out horse, wheeled into Stirrup's yard and was met at the steps by Wafer's black-browed segundo, Mose Wheptrun.

"What you doin' over here?"

"I got to see Wafer—"

"Ain't you been told enough times—"

"Never mind that. I'm washed up over there. All hell's tore loose and' she's made Stroud ramrod—"

"What's that?" Wafer said, coming up behind Craftner. "You claim she's hired Stroud?"

Craftner said, "By Gawd, it's the truth! She turned me out an' give that drifter my job. He told me to get my stuff an' start hikin'! Just like that—no notice or nothin'. Just plain ordered me right off the place. By cripes," he said angrily, "if it wasn't I was scared of upsettin' your plans—not knowin' no more'n I do about 'em—I'd of sure made that gun fighter hard to find! But I didn't want— Hell! He told me to grab—"

"He know you're connected with Stirrup?"

"You think that bastard confides in me? Hell," Craftner snarled, "if I knew what the—"

But Wafer had transferred his look to Wheptrun. "You deliver that note?"

"Sure I delivered it."

"Personal?"

"Put it right in her hand like you told me."

Wafer swung his eyes back to Craftner. "When'd this happen?"

"About the middle of the mornin'—"

"And it took you all this time to get here?"

"I'm damn lucky t' *be* here! Any time I don't suit—"

"Any time you don't suit," Wafer said, "you'll be planted. Now let's have the guts and quit beatin' the bushes."

Craftner took a long breath. "He never give me no chance to throw my hull on a hoss. I set off down the road like I was makin' for town. When I figured I'd gone far enough I cut around an' lit out for Boxed Circle. My hand—"

"I ain't worried about your hand," Wafer said.

"Well," Craftner scowled, "that damn drifter foxed me. He was slicker'n we give him credit for. I kept a eye on my backtrail an' never seen a thing till I got halfway up that damn mountain. I stopped a couple seconds to get hold of my wind, an' there he come on that gaunted roan. Follerin' my sign, he was, an' not wastin' no damn time on it neither.

"I reached the Boxed Circle camp an' found the boys in a crap game. I told them about Stroud an' we fixed up a deal to stop his clock, but Tularosa muffed it. I had him holed up in that brush with a rifle. The rest of us was waitin' strung out along the ridge just in case he got cute—which he did. Tularosa let go with his rifle an' missed him, an' Stroud went crashin' into the spruce. We cut him off, turned him—boxed him up in that pole corral.

"He was good as got then, but the boys' broncs was in it. We had trouble gettin' a bead on him. We dropped two of the broncs tryin' to keep him pinned back of a upright while Wimpy wormed into that east rim brush. An' we'd of had him then if Jess' damn hoss hadn't of went plumb crazy an' cut for the gate. Stroud nabbed him.

"We knocked the hoss down but Stroud wriggled clear an' got into the ragweed. We hadn't none of us suspicioned he wasn't alone but we found out different when we come onto that ridge. He must of had half the Three Sixes crew waitin' for us. I damn near got my hand tore off! Tularosa—"

"Just a minute," Wafer said, and shot a hard look at Wheptrun. "Mose, send Whitey up to Globe on the double. Tell him to stay up there an' keep his eye peeled for Stroud—Whitey knows what he looks like, he saw him at that dance. Tell him to fix things up with that cousin of his that handles long-distance calls. I've got my own ideas about that guy; and if he tries to get anyone on the phone I want to know who it is and what he says to them. Got it?"

Wheptrun nodded and hurried off to the bunkhouse.

"They've got to get up damned early to get ahead of Dan Wafer," the Stirrup boss said, and turned back to Craftner. "Anyone besides you get clear of that fracas?"

"It's Gawd's own wonder *I* got away. You never seen such a slaughter—"

"Good!" Wafer grinned. "He's played right into our hands. Unprovoked assault. Rustler raid pulled in broad daylight. We're going to pin Three Sixes' hide—"

"I wish you luck," Craftner said, "but count me out. Soon's you pay me what I got comin'—"

"Just leave it to me, Link. I'll take care of you. When Dan Wafer's your friend he's your friend all the way. You'll see this different in the morning; you've got a big bonus coming. You go over and have Mose take a look at that hand. And don't worry. Stroud's not going to bother you."

"You're damn right he ain't!"

Wafer grinned through the gloom. "Don't be an ass, Craftner. I've said I'll take care of you."

"Well—all right," Craftner said, and was wheeling to start for the bunkhouse when some new thought suddenly swung him around.

In the shadows his eyes looked enormous. He shoved a hand out before him. "My Gawd, Dan! Don't—"

The heavy bullet smashed him backward. The reflexed hinges of his knees let go and spilled him down the groaning steps. His hat fell off and wobbled on its brim while one spur rowell spun its final song.

13

LET THE DOG SEE THE RABBIT

THE emotions loosed in Stroud by that voice were too complex, too confused and frought with turbulence, to be accurately translated into words. What words can sort the bright reds of courage or dredge the depths of a man's despair?

Stroud knew that voice. It turned him utterly still while anger whipped new strength through tired arteries and danger cleared his mind of shock.

Chuck Murgatroyd stood behind him and a baffled look reshaped Stroud's cheeks. He could think of no reason why the man shouldn't fire; it was what most gun wranglers would have done in his place. He was puzzled that the man should have spoken at all.

"If you're waitin'," he said, "for me to dive for that iron—"

Murgatroyd said, "I can bag my turkeys any way I find them."

The admission coincided with Stroud's own impression. So what was he waiting for? To hear Stroud beg?

Stroud's glance, turned narrow, considered the dead shape before him with a new, more vital interest. This hardcase hadn't died of old age. He'd been shot—and precisely at the moment he'd intended shooting Stroud. Stroud hadn't done it. So Murgatroyd must have.

Stroud turned around then. "With dumdums?" he said.

"When you want to make sure that's a pretty good way."

"You leave some damn queer tracks."

"I find yours interestin' too."

"I don't get it," Stroud said. "I ride into that spread, rough you up, ruin your prospects. You've got your eye on Lee's daughter and I pull her eye away from you. You're in line for Craftner's job and I latch onto that, too. You ought to hate my guts."

"You ain't kiddin'."

"Then why didn't you let Craftner's gundogs finish me?"

"In the first place," Murgatroyd said, smiling thinly, "they weren't Craftner's gundogs; they were a part of Wafer's setup which is somethin' else again. In the second place Cindy needs you if she's to stand any chance of holdin' off Wafer."

Stroud shook his head. "I still don't get it. You move around too quiet to be honest—"

"Honesty's nothin' but a tagline for suckers. I'm in this game for all I can get—and I can put up with a hell of a lot if it promises to get me what I'm after. So let's spread our cards right out on the table."

Stroud considered him. "You want to make a deal."

"I want to make a deal."

"Just what are you after?"

"I'm going to let you figure that out for yourself. You want the girl so you'll do what you can for her. I'm willin' to string along on that basis. You've got to have help. You can't do it alone.''

"Don't make too sure of that.''

"You weren't doin' so much with this Boxed Circle setup. Where the hell would you be if I hadn't bought in?''

"And that's another queer thing,'' Stroud murmured.

"What's queer about that? I got told off this mornin' to ride this fence. I heard the shootin' an' come over.''

"And threw in on my side.''

"I told you about that.''

"You walked over the ground. You didn't leave much sign.''

Murgatroyd scowled. "You better pick up your iron.''

Stroud picked up the pistol, pulled the loads and knocked the dirt out. Murgatroyd went over and brought up his horse and Stroud's. "Is that straight, what you said about gettin' Link's job?''

Stroud thrust the reloaded gun in his holster. "Yeah.'' He told Murgatroyd about following Craftner.

Murgatroyd nodded. "I kind of figured he was workin' undercover for Wafer. It fits all right but there's so damn many angles—'' He broke off, again frowning, considering Stroud narrowly. "Craftner got away; that means he's headed for Stirrup. Are we makin' a deal?''

"I'm not in the habit,'' Stroud said, "of making deals with my eyes shut—''

"That's the way you'll make this one.''

"I see no reason for making it."

Murgatroyd said irritably, "Don't be a fool! How the hell far do you think you'll get solo?"

"And how far would I get—"

"You'll get a hell of a lot farther with my help than without it!"

"I'd like to know what you've got in the back of your head. If I make any deal with you I've got a right to know what your stake is in this—"

"You ain't got no right to a goddam thing! You come into this after the hand was dealt! When you pick up cards in another man's game—"

"That," Stroud said, "is what's botherin' you. I've picked up cards and I'm holding right onto them."

"An' you'd be buzzard bait if I hadn't stepped in—"

"I owe you something for that—"

"Then pay it!" growled Murgatroyd. "All I'm askin' is that you let me alone until we get clear of Stirrup. The girl can't beat Wafer without help. I can't beat him alone an' you can't either. Teamed up we might do it, so I'll back your play till we get him cut down—"

"And then?"

"You can go your way an' I'll go mine."

Stroud searched his cheeks. "What you want, then—"

"All I want out of you is a workin' agreement that we'll bury the hatchet till we get this thing whipped. I don't know what you've got against me, an' I don't give a damn, but I don't want to have to keep an eye out for you while I'm fightin' to keep Wafer from grabbin' this ranch."

Murgatroyd met Stroud's eye straightly.

Stroud looked straightly at him. "All right," he said, "I'll give you that. What are you givin' me on this deal?"

"I'll give you my help against Wafer. I'll give you my knowledge of this country and this setup—"

"What can you tell me about the girl's brother, Loosh?"

"That pipsqueak!" Murgatroyd snorted. "Don't put no trust in him or you'll end up shovelin' coal for old Nick. He ain't got no more backbone than a bullfinch."

"Where's he at?"

"Probably bedded down somewhere in town with some chippy. He don't count in this deal one way or the other."

"I wish I could be sure of that." Stroud told him about Wafer's note to Cindy. Took it out of his pocket and showed him.

Murgatroyd whistled. "It's the kind of thing that damn fool would do."

"Then you reckon Wafer's got the deadwood on him?"

"It could be a frame. I can tell you one thing, if it is it'll be a lulu. That guy never sleeps an' he can pick up more angles than a dog can fleas."

He moved over to his horse and, scowling, tightened a cinch. "I reckon Dan's got him," he muttered, finally straightening. "Loosh can't keep his damn hands off the pasteboards. Wouldn't be no trick to get him into a game an' wind yourself up with a bunch of his paper. Wafer could of done it, or one of his men could."

He stood awhile, frowning. "That's probably how they worked it. Then Wafer says to the kid, 'You got enough cash to buy up this paper?' An' of course Loosh ain't. So Wafer says, 'When your ol' man kicks off you'll own half of that ranch. What's the matter with askin' him for the money?' Naturally Loosh knows if Wafer shows that stuff to his father any chance he's got of comin' into the ranch is cooked right then. Wafer knows it, too. So he talks Loosh into movin' enough beef to make good his IOU's. That's about the way he worked it. He probably done it more than once.''

Stroud was willing to string along with that theory. From what he'd gathered from Lucinda that would be Loosh's speed. "You got any idea why Wafer wants Three Sixes?''

For a moment Stroud thought Murgatroyd's eyes had changed expression, but all the man said was, "Why does Cindy want it?''

"That's different. To her it's a home place. She was raised—''

"Could be the same way with Wafer. His ol' man once owned a good chunk of this spread. House is still standin' down on Twenty-Mile Creek—''

"There's more to it than that.''

Murgatroyd's face tipped up a wry and slanting grin. "I reckon there is. There's a lot of spilled blood an' some evenin' up mixed into it, not to mention Smilin' Dan's ambition. In his picture of himself the guy's a second John Chisum. I think he's got it in his mind to grab this whole damn basin.''

"What use would he find for sheep do you reckon?''

Murgatroyd's eyes winnowed down to slits. "Sheep!'' He gave a scornful bark. "Sheep's the last thing you'll find on any grass owned by Dan! It's a *cattle* king he wants—''

"They're comin' in," Stroud said. "I don't mean any two or three handfuls."

The moments dragged like a run-down watch. A sense of change howled across Stroud's nerve ends and Murgatroyd's eyes, long schooled in concealment, could not quite hide their look of shock.

He ran a tongue across stiff lips. "You sure?"

"Go look for yourself. The whole range southeast of town is one great blanket of blattin' woollies. I made out six bands. There may be more. Where you reckon they're bound for?"

"Three Sixes—"

"What I figured. Got any ideas?"

Softly, wickedly, Murgatroyd cursed.

"I can subscribe to that opinion," Stroud said, "but it ain't going to butter any bread for Cindy. We better see if we can line up some of these outfits—"

"Not a chance."

Stroud said patiently, "Not, perhaps, in any fight with Stirrup; but sheep— It's as much in their interests as it is to ours. Sheep don't eat by maps or compass. Once let them get in—"

"You can tell them that till you're blue in the face." Murgatroyd's tone, like his eyes, was bleak. "You won't get a damn one to lift a hand. They'll think it's a trick. They been used before." He said with a look of bitter disgust, "They'll stare at you like a bunch of dumb cows an' bank on their wire to—"

"That won't stop them."

"You can't tell them that." Murgatroyd scrinched his lips and spat. "I'd as soon waste my time with a bunch of fool hens as to try to deal with the churn-

116

twistin' plow-chasers that call theirselfs 'ranchers' in—''

"We've got to make them see the truth—''

"I'll leave that chore to you then. I've got more faith in a case of dynamite. A couple of sticks of TNT will do more good in about five seconds—''

Stroud said with his glance gone darkly thoughtful, "Who was roddin' Three Sixes when you hired on?''

"Craftner.''

"You never met Lockett?''

"What's he got to do with these sheep?''

"I was thinkin' of something else,'' Stroud said, limping over to the roan and tightening the girths. "Then you don't think Wafer is back of these sheep?''

"It don't look like a guy in the cattle business would ruin good range he expects to get hold of—''

"Maybe he's decided to go into sheep.''

Murgatroyd grunted. "What you fixin' to do?''

"There'll be a moon in about three hours,'' Stroud said. "I think it's time I had a look at Stirrup.''

"Figurin' to let the dog see the rabbit?''

Stroud showed a tired grin and climbed into the saddle.

IT was quite a spread.

Wafer's headquarters, with its big white house and whirling windmills, its stout corrals and plastered adobe outbuildings half shaded by wind-tossed cottonwoods, its chain of tanks with their priceless water stretching out in the distance like silver lakes, was one of the finest looking outfits in all Arizona.

Stroud wondered again where Wafer had got hold of

the money which had gone into setting him up in such style. He said as much to Murgatroyd who shook his head and allowed it hadn't all happened in one day.

"But he had to have money to start at all."

"It don't take much to buy out a homesteader. He got his start on the old Boscom place, accordin' to the way I've heard it," answered Murgatroyd. "After awhile he bought out a couple more and brought in a bunch of mismated cows. What you see down there wasn't nothin' but desert when Dan bought into it."

"You don't think someone's backin' him?"

In the moonlight Murgatroyd's face looked surprised. "Well," he said at last, "it's somethin' to think about. Pretty hard to see Wafer, though, as someone's hired hand. He don't have the cut for that kind of ranny. He's a lot too much of a pusher—Where you want to go now?"

"Let's take a look at that dam."

After fifteen minutes of riding Murgatroyd stopped his horse and put out a hand. He said in a voice he kept carefully lowered, "About a half mile more an' you can wash your eyes in it. We better step along careful—Wafer's no fool. He ain't leavin' that dam loose for prowlers to play with."

Stroud nodded.

Several minutes later Murgatroyd pulled up again, this time before a dark screen of dwarf cedar. "I'll hold your horse. Work into that brush an' look off to the right."

WHEN Stroud again climbed into the saddle nothing about his look or manner disclosed any part of what was in his mind. He seemed content to plow the other's wake and showed little interest in the nature of their surroundings.

Cruising steadily along between the red-barked pines Murgatroyd, reviewing what he knew of this man, allowed a growing dissatisfaction to warp the processes of his thinking. His wire-edged features became steadily more forbidding and, when they came out once more upon the tree fringed spur overlooking Stirrup's buildings, he suddenly growled: "What the hell kind of game are you playing?"

Wind flapped the faded scarf about Stroud's neck and where moonlight touched the tough planes of his cheeks there appeared a suggestion of sardonic amusement. "What kind of a game do you think I'm playing?"

"By God, I don't know, but there's somethin' about you that sticks in my craw! You ain't no cut an' run drifter! I been watchin' you, mister; your brand looks all right but the knife slipped someplace when they was carvin' your earmarks. I'd like to know what brought you into this country."

"I seem to recall," Stroud said, "that it was you who suggested we ride this trail together."

"That don't stop me from wonderin'. You ain't sidin' Three Sixes for the money you get out of it. I figured for awhile it was account of the girl but I can't quite sell myself on that notion, either. You're usin' that job to cover somethin' else."

"You ought to hire out that brain to the Pinkertons."

Murgatroyd said blackly, "Maybe I will."

"Maybe you already have," Stroud growled; and then, seeing the way the man's lips drew together, "What do you make of all the quietness down there?"

For another long moment Murgatroyd's look beat against him before with a grunt it finally dropped down to Stirrup. "I don't like it," he muttered. "Damn place looks deserted."

"My thought, too. Maybe we better be ridin'."

"Maybe we had," Murgatroyd said grimly.

14

HARD CHOICE

A TRIFLE, sometimes, can change the whole course of empire. The shape of a smile, a whispered word, the compassion glimpsed in a woman's eyes.

The world sets a lot of store by trifles but it was something primitive, more intangible and urgent, that was hurrying Stroud through the moonlit reaches of this tumultuous night. Lunging through the cross-hatched maze of light and shadow with the wind off the crags full and cold upon their faces, and the wind of their travel closing out every sound but the rattaplan rhythm of pistoning hoofs, he was filled with a strange unaccountable fear.

Mood, he told himself irritably—a natural depression brought about by what he'd been through, by nervous exhaustion or loss of blood and temper in the wounds he had gathered during that fight at Boxed Circle.

But the feeling hung on, amounting almost to conviction.

Was there something he'd forgotten? Some illusive thread of memory which, continuing to chafe, lay buried in the troubled depths of a mind which hadn't rested since the night he'd opened that cabin door on the Santa Cruz an hour's ride north of Tubac? His wounds, now cleansed and bandaged, were hardly of a nature to invite hallucination.

It was premonition, obviously; a grim foretaste of calamity. What he could not understand was why it should hit him so sharply now. Was it derived from sight of those blatting sheep? Was it something to do with Lockett or Craftner? Had it sprung from something in connection with Cindy, with her unstable brother or that prodigal uncle who had managed his resurrection barely in time to attend her father's funeral? Had it to do with something glimpsed but forgotten in the character or person of Beulah May? Or did it stem directly from some hardly noticed act or word emanating from that land-hungry pirate, Wafter?

Stroud cursed beneath his breath and used the steel with increasing frequency, sending the panting roan through the shadows with a reckless disregard of drops which at last jerked from Murgatroyd an irascible protest.

"You'll be no good to anyone at the bottom of a gulch with your head bashed in! Pull up, you fool, till I get my breath!"

Stroud reduced the gelding's pace to a lope and the gun fighter growled, "What the hell's eatin' on you?"

"I've got a feelin' we're going to get there too late."

"Too late for what? An' get where?"

"If I had the answer to that—"

"If it's them damn sheep—"

"I don't know," Stroud sighed; but deep in his bones he was afraid he did.

God knew he had reason enough to hate sheep. And experience enough with sheepmen's ways to know for what little time he could hope to block them. All he could honestly expect to do was to keep the sheep off the upper range until the conservationists got their bill through—if, indeed, they should be so lucky. That bill was on the floor right now and a decision could be expected within the next few days.

It would be a mighty dumb sheepman who didn't know this—they were fighting it tooth and toenail. If the bill went through this would all be a part of the proposed National Forest and it was a well known fact that the present Chief Forester was unalterably opposed to anything which even so much as smelled like a sheep. It was obvious, then, that this current invasion might have nothing to do with the feud between Wafer and Cindy's Three Sixes. It may have had its inception in some sheep pool's hope of establishing previous usage; yet this, in itself, did not mitigate Stroud's responsibility.

The sheep could be back of everything he felt. Yet could he reasonably say that some portion of this feeling was not tied up with Loosh? With some underlying feeling of guilt or inadequacy? Hadn't Wafer's ultimatum been plain enough, and hadn't he in becoming Three Sixes' ramrod ignored it?

He was faced with a task which might daunt any man and which few, less desperate, would have undertaken. He had had no right to add the burden of Cindy's problems to his own, no right to even think of a woman with a fate worse than death hanging so insecurely over him.

But life was so swift and so hard to let go of.

The grip of Stroud's fingers bit into the reins, the line of his jaw going granite hard. Life didn't care what was camped on your trail, what was back of your thoughts or what was in your heart even. Life was an inveterate joker, a Nero fiddling while watching Rome burn, a mischievous child hiding back of a purse with a thread tied onto its twister.

Life had shown him Cindy getting off her black horse before the store at Thief River.

And now he was trapped again, caught irrevocably.

He clenched his fists till the bones of his hands shone white in the moonlight. And again he swore beneath his breath, for how could he do this thing to that girl? She was not like Vingie. She was clean and sweet as a prairie rose.

He'd had no real intention of going out to her ranch, knowing well what kind of trouble lagged along just back of his bootsteps. Yet he had gone, piling iniquity onto folly with all a profligate's abandon—letting her hope where he could see no hope, allowing her to pin her faith on a man whose tomorrows had been traded away for the smile on a harlot's lips.

But her need had been so critically urgent, and he had not known there was no hope then—that was why he'd gone to Three Sixes. It was why he'd taken the job she'd offered, thinking what help he could give might perhaps stall things off till she could get better aid; but that had been folly. Things were moving too fast. She had no time now to scout other aid, and where would she be when the past caught up with him? For catch up it would if he stayed around here. He had no doubt at all about that part.

He could forgive himself mistakes like these; under

similar conditions any man might have made them. What he guessed he never would get out of his craw was that, realizing her trust, he had not seen where that dependence might take her. He had not dreamed that love might be its logical development; and when love had come, when she had squarely faced him, holding herself fully open to him, offering herself without reserve proudly, he had misunderstood—had been too blind to see it.

He had been unable to believe his luck and gave fervent thanks to God for that now, blessing Beulah May for the interruption which had driven them apart before any act or words of his had led him to commit something worse than folly.

He had no right to her love—less right to return it. Only a rogue would accept what she offered with the fate of Mike Stroud hanging over his head.

He could not deny the hunger that ran like a white hot flame through the core of his being. But he could bear it in silence as he had borne other things—must school himself to bear it, for her sake. Better far that she believe herself scorned than engulfed by the misery of the miserable truth. For what could he say—what comfort give—when the hounds of the law rode into her yard to drag him back to Yuma Prison, for life?

"HAVE you any idea of what we're up against here?" Murgatroyd spoke out of a long riding silence. "Any plans—any notions?"

"I'm going to try to get the small outfits to help us."

"They won't do it. Three Sixes has been top dog too long and the small boys haven't lapped up enough gravy. They're ripe for a change. Wafer's played his cards well. What will you do when they refuse to help you—have you thought about that?"

"You seem to have," Stroud said, and Murgatroyd snorted.

"Why else would I be stringin' along? Not out of love for you, by God! I'm playin' your game because I've run out of chips. Because I can't see anything else to do."

"Not a thing?"

Murgatroyd flung him a look, said testily, "I'm not that hard up for ideas! We could blow up his dam, but what the hell good would that do? Water's not the main issue; it's important, but not right now. I could burn down his place but that wouldn't help either. The main problem, the basic problem as I see it, is to find some means to stop Wafer. I can—"

"You've put your finger on something but you're forgettin' the sheep—"

"First things first—"

"The first thing may be Wafer," Stroud said, "but a ruined range ain't going to help Cindy. If you don't know what sheep do I can tell you. By the time those sheep have got through with her grass—"

"Hell, I know all that! The Forest Reserve Bill—"

"We can't wait on that bill. This grass is threatened *now*. Not tomorrow or next week but right now, and you know it; so it's not Cindy's grass you're worried about." Stroud looked at him slanchways. "If you harm one hair of that girl's head—"

"No one's fixin' to hurt her—"

"No one better be!"

They rode more than a mile without further talking, Stroud holding the pace to a ground-eating lope. Then

Murgatroyd said, "Sink, swim or swaller, we're in this together an' we better be figurin' out what we're goin' to do. If you've got any ideas, let's hear them."

"I sort of had the notion you'd found a way to stop Wafer."

"Stoppin' him's easy. It's what happens afterwards that's got me stumped."

Stroud thought about that, and he kept on thinking. After another quarter mile he couldn't endure it any longer. He said, "If you know how to stop him . . ."

Murgatroyd grinned. "Ain't your ramrod's mind figured that out yet? Stoppin' him's simple. All it requires is a gun and a little nerve."

"I'm surprised you haven't done it."

Murgatroyd's mouth curled away from his teeth. "The trouble is with me, I've got too much imagination. There's a string to that sugarplum—Wafer don't ride alone. The gent that drops Dan Wafer is goin' to get dropped right beside him."

15

ONE CRACK OF LIGHT

WHATEVER was to be done would have to be done quickly. The note Lee had signed, to get money to keep going, was secured by a mortgage and would have to be met. This was not the best season for marketing beef but there was always the chance the people holding the note might be talked into extending its coverage. If they would not, Stroud would have to start rounding up cattle. This would require every hand on Three Sixes' payroll, hands urgently needed right now for other work. The nearest market they could count on was Prescott, at least a twenty days' drive. A long time to leave Three Sixes unprotected.

And there was Wafer to be considered. The man would not remain idle. And there was Loosh.

Stroud said, "We've got to find Loosh."

"We ought to've looked for him at Stirrup. We had a good—"

"You game to go back now?"

"I'll go back," Murgatroyd said finally, "but I won't guarantee anything beyond that. Time to've done our lookin'—"

"I know," Stroud nodded, and said without rancor, "Just do what you can."

Murgatroyd eyed him peculiarly a moment, then pulled his horse around and without further words set out over the backtrail. Stroud watched him go. Then he put the gaunt roan into motion again.

Desire to inflict bodily damage was in him, a self recriminatory mood given impetus by the rise of dark fancies sprung from an increasing appreciation of his own inadequacy. A kind of guilt complex, some might have called it; and he was, in all truth, bitterly aware of his guilt. Because he had aroused fear in Wafer, and suspicion, the Stirrup boss had been moved to exploit his hold over Loosh in that grim ultimatum he had served on Cindy. Because Stroud had ignored this— had persuaded the girl to, anything which happened to Loosh would be his fault. He was doubly responsible because, by his own reasoning, he had placed Loosh at Stirrup and yet had failed to search Stirrup when the chance had been given him. That other concerns had crowded Loosh from his thoughts was small excuse.

In this mood of self castigation Stroud was minded to assume responsibility for all the evils of the country— and why, indeed, shouldn't he? Was he not, in fact, a blight which ruined everything it touched? A boomerang to every man or woman who sought to use him? Hadn't he learned long ago that what a man had inside him was not altered by his whereabouts? How could he have thought to help Cindy when the record plainly showed he could not even help himself?

Hopelessly his weary mind went round the bitter circle. The note that was coming due. The beef that had to be gathered, trailed and marketed to provide the cash to meet the note which might have to be met to stave off foreclosure. The need of patrols to protect the ranch's wire. The need of other patrols to ward off the depredations of Stirrup. Stroud's own personal problems—the need which had gaunted the roan he bestrode and which was grown more acute with each passing hour. The problem of Loosh and the effect and involvements, should it be carried out, of Wafer's threat to expose Loosh Lee as the man at the back of this rustling. Stroud's relationship with Cindy and now, on top of everything else, those sheep.

Doggedly Stroud went over these things. Counting himself he had but four men to work with, none of whom, as he knew, could have held down a job with any outfit which valued the good opinion of its neighbors. Four men.

They were not enough to work a range and trail a herd to market. Normally perhaps, if time weren't so desperately against him, it might be done. But how could he leave the ranch unguarded with sheep even now within sight of its grass? How could he expect four men to get a herd through to Prescott with Stirrup so hungrily watching every move?

He'd be lucky even to get a beef herd gathered.

He couldn't do it. There was no way to cut it short of having more help or more time if not both. Four men couldn't even hold back the sheep. There was no use trying to fool himself. The men with those sheep would be Chihuahua Mexicans, a breed long inured to hardship and killing, turned ruthless in the yoke of rich hidalgos. They would come armed with rifles and riding fast horses, their bellies well filled with slaughtered beef.

Stroud knew them well. They were afraid of nothing and would cross any deadline cowmen set. And why not? Didn't the laws protect them? Deadlines were illegal and, so long as they kept to the open range, they could shoot any cowman who stuck out his jaw. And if their sheep broke down a few fences—well, what could you expect with all that shooting going on?

Sheep was big business these days with lobbies in Washington, relatives in offices, friends on the benches and mutton eaters packing every jury that was called. They had a vast and effective organization with large cash reserves in the biggest banks, and the only instruction ever given a herder was "Feed my sheep!" The owners didn't say how or give a damn. They equipped each pelado with a good grade of pistol, all the food he could swallow, a horse with bottom and a .45-90 rifle. They had the same answer for everything—first the bullets and then the law courts, and any cowman lucky enough to beat both was glad to get out of the country.

This was what Stroud was faced with—Stroud, who had learned the hard way about sheep. Which was why Jeff Douglas had picked him.

EVERYTHING had been most secret, even to his removal from Marshal Gilliflores' custody. That had happened at night at San Miguel which they'd reached by roundabout trails through the mountains, the argument being that the sheep crowd would probably waylay them if they took the most direct route to Yuma. It was 9:15 without benefit of moon when they'd pulled up in front of the Santa Rosa Restaurant, less than five miles from the Mexican border. Leaving their tired horses at the hitchrack, fully in view through the hash house window, they had all tramped inside, Stroud, the marshal and the marshal's two helpers.

Just after the waitress had gone off with their orders, the marshal had expressed an urge to visit the can; Stroud, his right hand manacled to Gilliflores' left, perforce going with him. The "gents" at the Santa Rosa occupied a cubbyhole back of the kitchen and was reached by traversing a long and narrow hall. Two doors opened off it, one leading to their destination, the other marked "ladies."

Once the door had shut behind them the marshal lost no time in freeing Stroud. "Window's kind of small," he said, "but I reckon you can make it. You'll find an alley outside and a saddled horse. In half an hour you should be over the line—"

"You're turnin' me *free*?"

"Free as a bird—an' you better fly like one if you don't want to catch a hunk of lead through your briskett. You're escapin', see? Once across the line you'll head directly for Nogales. You should be there by mornin'. You're to locate a leather worker, Tio Esteban, who has a place in the street of the silver merchants. Ask there for the American."

"Who's to keep me from goin' straight south?"

"Not a thing. Not one damn thing, boy, except your conscience. It's between you and God—now get goin'."

At ten o'clock the next morning Stroud presented himself at the shop of Tio Esteban and asked for the American. The wrinkled mummy working over a yellow saddle grunted through a mouthful of nails, gesturing indifferently toward a door at the rear. Stepping through that door Stroud walked into the cold scrutiny of Jeff Douglas.

"Stroud?" Douglas said.

Stroud nodded.

"I've a job for you." The man's sharp eyes made a swift appraisal. "A job that requires a desperate man, which is one of the reasons you're standing here. An escaped convict found guilty of murder and sentenced to Yuma for the rest of his life should be desperate enough for most anything."

Stroud's mouth shaped a lean, unhumorous smile. The blue of his stare looked as chilled as a well chain. "I guess," he said, "you know what you're doin'."

The Chief Forester said dryly, "Considering the bother I've been to, I hope so." He wiped the sweat off his jowls and went on to explain how Forest Reserves were designed to conserve natural resources; wildlife, timber, watersheds. "Moneyed interests, long accustomed to a ruthless exploitation of these resources, do not want government controls which will naturally put some kind of a curb on the amount of dollars they can continue to steal from the public inheritance. These interests are doing everything in their power to make sure no further land areas are set aside for this purpose.

"The President, who has lived out here, understands the small fellow's problems; he knows that if current conditions are allowed to continue this whole western country will become one vast desert. He has no intention of letting that happen. We have a bill up now to save the Salt River watershed by the establishment of another National Forest. This bill will not ruin the big cattlemen. It will not ruin the lumbermen. It *will* succor hundreds of small-spread ranchers who would otherwise be wiped out. Don't you think that's a job worth doing?''

"You didn't get me over here to learn what I think."

The Chief Forester smiled. "That's right. So now we come to the sheep. I don't have to tell *you* how destructive sheep are. As you've probably heard, I'm pulling every string I can get my hands on to keep them out of the National Forests. The sheepmen know this—they don't want any more National Forests. They don't give a damn about posterity; they don't want to own land. If they have to they will lease it but they don't want to have to. They're fighting us just as hard and as dirty as they fight cattlemen—''

"Suppose you come to the point."

Douglas nodded. "A lot of this fighting's being done in the legislature but the bloody end of it'll be done right here. In Arizona—in country we want set aside as a Forest. It won't be pretty. It's not a thing I would ask any man to buck, and I'm not asking you. I'm going to give you a choice."

He got a cigar from his pocket, bit the end off, watching Stroud with those reticent eyes.

"As you're probably aware, the biggest sheepmen around here are the McClannigans, Slade and Angus. Not many people around these parts have ever seen Slade, to know him. But I have reason to believe he was the brains of the combine. A shrewd politician, Slade dreamed up the angles, took care of the fixing, made contacts. A born actor who has made palm-crossing pay off in seven figures."

Douglas lit his cigar, puffed, said impatiently, "Well? You know him, don't you?"

Cords of muscle stood out along Stroud's clamped jaws. "I'd know him if I saw him, I suppose," he said at last. "When his crowd sheeped me out of the cow business, Slade was reckoned to be in California someplace—"

"I have reason to believe he's in the Superstitions now. When you killed Angus, Slade ducked for cover. I want him flushed out. I want him tied up with his dirty work in a way that will give the law a chance to get hold of him.

"I have used some extremely unorthodox methods to have this little talk with you. In a desperate situation, desperate expedients sometimes have to be used. This job calls for a man who can use a gun, who will know Slade when he sees him and who will not be disposed to listen if money should get to talking.

"You," Douglas told him bluntly, "are the only man available who fills all three requirements. You're on the dodge and you'll remain a hunted convict till the doors of Yuma Prison close behind you. This job I want done guarantees you nothing, gives you no protection. Every man's hand will be against you. If caught, you will be taken to Yuma, as sentenced, there remaining for so long as you live, given every penalty accorded an escaped prisoner."

Douglas looked at his watch; said abruptly: "Regardless of what you may decide to do, when you step out of this room you will be strictly on your own. I exact no promises. If you want to run for it you can run."

Stroud's set face showed a startled expression, a look that was almost incredulous. "Man, you're layin' yourself wide open!"

"I've already done that." The Chief Forester con-

135

sidered him gravely. "I'm a pretty good judge of character, Stroud. I don't think you'll run."

STROUD lifted his shoulders, let them fall. What could he do—what could *any* man do where the deck was stacked and the odds piled so high against him? There was a limit to human endurance. Too many things needed doing at once and he hadn't enough of anything. Too few men and too little time.

He let the roan down to a shambling walk, the last bit of urgency drained from his system. He knew when he was licked; there was no way out and that was all there was to it. The wall of odds was too high; there was no hole anyplace, not a damn crack! Wafer held every trump in this game and Slade McClannigan, if he was in this country, was lying so low hell itself couldn't find him.

What chance had an ant, Stroud asked himself bitterly, in a jungle shaken by the roar of elephants?

He was filled with an overpowering sense of futility, strangled on the dregs of despair. But his mind worked on, still casting about for a glimmer of light, for one tiny crevice—for one bit of flesh he could get his teeth into. And, incredibly, he found one; a simple matter of viewpoint, a question of relationship he hadn't properly channeled. On his feet, still conceding himself a chance, he hadn't been able to see the woods for the trees. Now, at the rocky bottom of his last expiring hope, the matter of those sharp-hoofed, sharp-teethed sheep revealed themselves capable of a different interpretation.

He'd been hooking them up with the ruin of Three

Sixes but, forgetting that aspect of their appearance, didn't they present a broad arrow pointing straight toward the whereabouts of Slade McClannigan? Of course they did! It was so damned obvious he'd never given it a thought, but who else had that many sheep at his disposal? And he'd been wondering all this time where Dan Wafer had gotten his money!

It was plain enough now.

McClannigan, who must have long been aware of Douglas' convictions concerning sheep, would have foreseen the current trend in procedures and would have taken steps to protect himself against the encroaching threat of additional National Forests. He would have tied up with key men all over the West where large areas of public lands were likely to be set aside in the interests of conservation; men such as Wafer to whom there were no gods sacred and whose driving ambitions Slade would know how to use.

Stroud's mind, gone to work in grim earnest, commenced going over the probabilities with a patient care which overlooked no detail. And, gradually, his whole terrain of thought began shifting. The road blocks were still up but, in several instances, boggy detours were discernible where before there had been nothing but black craters of despair. Angle after angle now disclosed new facets until the whole scale of values revealed the need of revision.

There was only one way the McClannigans could make sure of feeding their sheep on National Forests. That was to show previous usage of those lands by sheep. Up until now their flocks had been gorging themselves on the open range, stealing their way across land held by cattlemen. But a man shrewd as Slade would long since have deciphered the writing on the wall.

If he had dealt with Wafer for a right of way through the Thief River country, southeastern boundary of the proposed Crook National, he must have provided whatever cash had been needed to build Wafer into a size which could now guarantee whatever he had paid for.

But suppose with Wafer's rise the man's ambition had risen also until now it envisioned complete domination of the Thief River region? Yeasty with pride and strong now in fire power, would he still be willing to allow sheep passage through what he must regard as being virtually his kingdom? If he let the sheep through—if he kept to the bargain he must have made with McClannigan—then he certainly wasn't obsessed with grabbing range for the use of cattle.

If it wasn't for cattle, what *did* he want range for? Sheep? Well, possibly, Stroud conceded, but he could not make himself put any faith in it.

And where was Slade McClannigan hiding? Was he holed up at Stirrup? Was McClannigan perhaps the outfit's real owner and Wafer nothing more than a kind of super-ramrod?

Stroud greatly doubted that a man of Wafer's gumption could long be content with playing front for another. And where was Lockett—the man whose sudden departure had made it possible for Craftner to help the burly Wafer crucify Three Sixes? Lockett's disappearance looked a bit too opportune not to be part and parcel of the rest of this business.

There were a lot of strange conjectures rolling round

inside Stroud's noggin, and one or two were pointed toward becoming real suspicions.

Very probably, he mused, Murgatroyd and Cindy were quite right in believing that most of the smaller owners would not budge from their fences to help the Lees in any fuss with Wafer. Murgatroyd also was very likely correct in assuming they would make no attempt to stop the sheep. But he had found long ago that no good ever came of relying on others' opinions. If you wanted the truth you'd better dig it out yourself; and the truth right now was that Stroud needed help.

16

BRUSH POKER

THE morning was half spent when Stroud came into the yard at Three Sixes with four other men, took a quick look around and reined his horse to a stop where Banjo Bill and Shampoo Charlie sat leisurely whittling in the shade of the cottonwoods.

"What the hell you guys think you're doin'?"

The pallid faced dwarf cringed away from Stroud's look but the cadaverous Charlie, with a shrug, answered mildly, "Jest follerin' orders."

"*Whose* orders? Craftner's not roddin' this spread any more. Di—"

"We got our orders straight from Mister Lee."

"Lee? Lee's dead!"

"Well, now . . . Sure enough?" Charlie flexed his back and chucked a glance at his companion. "You hev any trouble hearin' Mister Lee, Banjo?"

Stroud said, "You talkin' about *Loosh?*"

The cadaverous Charlie scrinched up his eyes, looked it over from several angles and finally shook his head. "I can't make out what Loosh has got t' do with it. Miz' Cindy's unc—"

"Oh! *That* Lee! Didn't Cindy tell you—"

"We ain't seen Miz' Cindy. Mister Lee allowed as how she'd gone up to Phoenix. Said he reckoned we had better stick aroun' till she got back."

"All right. I'll have a talk with him—"

"You'll hev t' go t' town then. He drove off in his rig a couple or three hours ago. That woman he brung with him is—here she comes now."

Stroud had already seen her. He said, "Where's Murgatroyd?"

"Your guess is as good as mine," Charlie shrugged. "He rode in here this mornin' aroun' five o'clock. When he found you wasn't round he cut him out a fresh bronc an' went larrupin' off."

"Stroud," Beulah May began, "I—"

"In a minute," Stroud said, and addressed himself to the hunchback. "I've been given the job of runnin' this ranch. In the future—startin' now—you'll take your orders from me. Is that clear?"

The hunchback, licking dry lips, silently nodded.

"All right, then," Stroud said harshly. "We've got no time to be sittin' around whittlin'. I want a beef herd rounded up. I want it ready for trailing inside of five days. You're the boss, Banjo; these boys are goin' to help you and I want you to remember they're only hired to work cattle. They're not hired to work a gun. Now grab a horse and get goin'."

"What about grub?"

Stroud waved him away. "You're the boss." He turned hard eyes on the rawboned Charlie. "You're goin' with them. Cram your pockets full of cartridges and take the fastest horse you can find on the place. Your job's to make sure that gather's not bothered. If anything shapes up to be more than you can handle, you come after me—and you come a-runnin'.''

He swung around then, grim stare focusing a picture of the girl. Black hair made an attractive arrangement beneath the broad brim of her chin-strapped white Stetson. Full breasts pushed out the front of her shirtwaist; trim hips gave style to a divided skirt of yellow corduroy. Two of the men he had fetched here with him were openly exhibiting a frank approval and someway, unaccountably, this irritated Stroud. Beulah May had a quirt looped round a wrist and he thought, very briefly, to have caught a flash of fear in her eyes; but that, of course, was sheer nonsense. There was no reason why she should be frightened.

He said curtly: ''Well?'' and she considered him a moment before red lips pulled away from white teeth and abruptly quirked at their corners.

''My! Do you always scowl when you talk to a woman?''

''Sorry,'' Stroud said. ''I've got a lot on my mind.''

''I'm sure you must have,'' the red lips smiled. ''I'm to tell you Cindy's gone off to Phoenix to try and get those people to give her more time. She hopes to be back here sometime tomorrow.''

''When did she go?''

''We had the funeral right after lunch and Cindy left right after the funeral—yesterday.''

Stroud stood a moment thinking out a course of action. He said, ''What did your father go to town for this morning?''

''He's been worrying about Cindy. He's such a chivalrous old dear, and terribly afraid she's going to lose the old homestead. He's gone to see if he can't arrange a little loan to tide her over.''

"I thought he had come here figurin' to get a loan himself."

"Well, he had," Beulah May said candidly. "But he'd naturally supposed Uncle Cy was doing well. When he discovered the truth he was awfully upset."

She looked at Stroud brightly. "That's one thing about us Lees, we believe in sticking together. Dad wanted to rush back home and sell out all his holdings but Uncle Cy wouldn't hear of it. He said he guessed he'd squeeze by. . . . You don't happen to know where Loosh is, do you?"

Stroud shook his head. "I've got a man out looking for him." He tilted his head, cocked a glance at the sun. "Then your dad isn't dependent on his patent medicine business?"

Her eyes opened wide and then she gave a little laugh. "Good lord—he just does that for amusement! Dad's considered one of the richest men in Tonopah—"

"Then why would he be tryin' to get a loan from Cindy's father?"

"That's quite a long story. Dad has got his fingers in a good many kinds of business—rather too many I would imagine from what he's said."

Her eyes, suddenly crinkling, made a kind of joke between them, and once more her little laugh tinkled across the morning stillness. "I guess I'm not very smart about business, but I believe it's called 'over-extending.' Anyway, he has a chance to make quite a killing. But, to do this, he has to put up ten thousand dollars. He can't scrape it up without selling out some of his other interests. He's afraid, if he should try to do that, it would cause some kind of a panic or other and wipe out all of his holdings. So he hit on the idea of borrowing it from Cyrano.''

"Yet he thinks he might fix up a loan for Cindy?''

"That's not at all the same thing. Cindy doesn't—''

"Well, it's very kind of him," Stroud said, "but if he really wants to be of some help you tell him not to give out any more orders to the crew. One boss around here is enough at a time.''

Touching his hat, then, he left her, moving over to the corral where, dismounting, he pulled the gear from his horse, draping the damp blanket hair-side up across his saddle. He watched the roan paw the ground for a moment, go around in a circle and commence to fold up. He did not look at the girl again, thus missing the expression with which she stared after him. He waited until the gaunt roan began to roll, then went to the barn and got a measure of oats.

When he came back the horse was still rolling, getting the saddle kink out of its spine. Stroud watched him get up and shake himself. Then he gave him the oats and went after some hay.

God, but he was weary. He would have liked nothing better than to fall into a bunk and sleep the clock around. He supposed he had probably ought to look at his wounds again, but he couldn't spare the time to do that right now, either.

He gave the roan his hay, got his rope from the saddle and, going into the pen where the cavvy was held, snaked out the baldfaced grulla he'd caught yesterday and got him ready to ride. Then he climbed aboard and rode over to the cookshack where Go Slow, the halfbreed Papago, fixed him up a cold lunch that he could eat in the saddle. Munching on this he set off for town.

He remembered the sound of Beulah May's laughter, the shape of her smile, the snug fit of her getup, and found himself wondering how many of these things she might have studied for their effect. She didn't seem at all to be that kind of a girl and he couldn't think where he had picked up the impression, but he more than half suspected Beulah May was on the prowl.

He forgot the girl entirely when he caught his first sight of town. The warped and time-bleached hitchracks were crowded with tied horses and a dark smell of trouble hung over the place. Knots of men stood along its walks in grim silence and other groups stood glowering in the shade of the pink-barked pines. All had their eyes fixed across the river where a blatting gray line of hungry sheep were moving steadily deeper into the heart of cow country.

There were eight or ten herders in sight at the moment and they were a hard looking lot, well mounted. All their duffle was packed on burros and mules, and these were up near the front of the line between the first band and the second. Two men rode point near the head of the column which was pouring into the cedar brakes four miles north of town; the rest were strung out through the billowing dust churned up from those thousands of black cutting hoofs. As far as Stroud could see to the south the dust rose and hung in the quiet air. It was a full scale invasion, no doubt about that.

Stroud stopped his grulla near the first group of cowmen who looked around at him briefly with dark hostile glances before resuming their sullen regard of the sheep. Nobody spoke or paid him further attention.

He looked around for Redcliff but did not see him, nor did he see the rig of Beulah May's father. Two of the sheepmen sat their dust-coated horses on the bank of the river directly across from the place where Stroud watched. They were big burly men with a scraggle of beard on their dark sunburnt faces. Both wore black hats, faded cotton shirts and scuffed chaparejos. They wore heavy work shoes instead of boots. Each of them showed a belted pistol and an efficient looking rifle of the repeater variety was conspicuously scabbarded on each of the double-rigged saddles.

Stroud looked again at that near group of ranchers. Their eyes held a deep and sullen resentment but nothing of the fury which breeds retaliation. These were men without hope, already beaten, cowed by the fate of other cowmen. They would not interfere; there was not one ounce of fight in the bunch of them.

Lips curled with contempt, he turned his back on them and sent the big grulla toward the bed of the river, splashing him through the shallow pools of stagnant water, driving him up the farther bank with the hatred of months laying bright in his stare.

Reining in before the pair of black-hatted horsebackers, "Good morning," he said, holding hard to his temper. "Which one of you fellers is in charge of these sheep?"

They both looked him over with their mouths full of tobacco and the younger one grinned. The stockier man sent a stream of amber spittle splashing over the rocks, crammed another hunk of black twist in his mouth and chomped it awhile with a winkless attention.

"I am," he said, pulling his gun around front, "an' if it's trouble you're huntin' you can get it right here. Name's Smith—Cheyenne Smith, an' my advice to you is to let well enough alone."

Stroud digested this in silence, pondering a remark Jeff Douglas had made in the shop of the leather carver. *In a desperate situation*, the Chief Forester had said, *desperate expedients sometimes have to be used*. Stroud considered it probable this was such an occasion.

He crossed his hands on the horn of the saddle where they were in plain sight and said nervously, "Would you mind ridin' over that trail again? I don't hear right good since I been bored fer the simples."

The younger man sniggered. Smith's hard eyes went over Stroud again while Stroud showed what he hoped would be taken for the look of a halfwit. Apparently it was, for the sheep boss, grimacing, waved a calloused grimy hand in an all-inclusive gesture. "You see how we're holdin' them sheep in line? It's entirely up to me whether we keep 'em that way. Instead of tramplin' down the graze in a quarter-mile swath I could just as easy move these bands eight abreast an' clean this country plumb down to bedrock—which is what I will do if I get any sass from you goddam cowprodders. Now get the hell outa here an' get out quick!"

" 'F you're goin' to talk like that I sure will, mister. I was only figurin' to be a little neighbor—"

"No knotheaded cow walloper's goin' to run it over *me!*"

"Well, cripes a'mighty! I'm no cowman—ain't even got a job no more! I been cookin' fer the Randymier outfit but they give me the sack. That's some of their crowd standin' over across the river.''

Smith loosed a snort and another load of brown tobacco. ''Bunch of cold-footed bastards if I ever seen any.''

''Hell, them fellers is just floaters—extra roundup hands they was figurin' to turn loose of till they got wind of you gents comin' up with these sheep. They're just waitin' around now prayin' you boys'll cross the river; their pay starts again the minute anything with wool on climbs that farther bank.''

''Oh, it does, eh?'' Cheyenne Smith curled back his lips. ''An' then what happens?''

''They just stay where they are till you get all these sheep moved into the foothills—that's when the fun starts. Ol' Randy's fixin' to make a example of you. He's holed up back in the brush along Three Sixes south fence with fifteen handpicked slug slammers straight from Dodge City an' Tombstone. He says when he gets through with you there won't another damn sheepman ever come near this country.''

The burly sheep boss glared like he was minded to push Stroud's face in. ''If you think that kind of crap is goin' to scare—''

''What would *I* be wantin' to scare you fer? I wouldn't ask nothin' better'n to see you fellers blast that bunch clean to hell an' gone. Now that you know what they're cookin' up for you an' where they're aimin' to pull the deal off—''

''How'd your shirt get clawed up? What you got them rags tied around you for?''

Stroud pulled off one of the bandages and showed

him. "Them damn gun fighters done that. The ol' man sicced 'em onto me when I opened my jaw about him not payin' me my money—by cripes, I was lucky t' git away from there alive!"

Smith looked at the other man. "What you think, Dove? Is this guy tellin' the truth?"

The younger sheepman said, "Why take a chance? It ain't goin' to slow us much to—"

"Slade told us—"

"He said he had it all fixed, that there wouldn't be no opposition— How do we know he ain't been double-crossed?"

"We could probably get through—"

"He ain't goin' to like it if we lose a bunch of these sheep."

The burly Smith scowled blackly. Stroud said, "You could probably get through now you know what you're up against. Of course he's got some scouts out but—"

"What are those birds across the river figurin' to do after we get the sheep started into the foothills?"

"You can't prove it by me. I didn't get invited to set in on no details. All I know is what I've told you. He's got fifteen gunslingers bedded in the brush along Three Sixes' south fence an' these fellers across the river gets back on his payroll soon's the first of your bunch hits the other side."

Dove said: "I don't like it! There's a weasel got into this woodpile someplace—how the hell did this Randymier get next to us anyway? How'd he know we was goin' through Three Sixes?"

Smith said, "What about takin' this guy along—"

"Not me!" Stroud growled. "I don't want no part of it!"

"If I'd been shot at—"

"That's why I tipped you off. But you don't catch me messin' around with Drik Randymier—that ol' pelican means business. He's a pal of Dan Wafer's an', between 'em, they just about run this country."

He observed the quick look that passed between the two sheepmen. "You do anything you want to, boys, but just count me out. I'm gettin' shed of this country by the shortest route."

And, picking up his reins, he moved the grulla on past them into the dust of the sheep, heading south.

17

CURTAIN CALL

IT was after three o'clock when Stroud once again rode into Three Sizes' yard, pulled off the saddle and rubbed down the lathered grulla. He got the horse some hay without seeing anyone.

He went over to the water tub, pulled off his torn shirt and gave himself a bath from the waist on up. Then he looked at his wounds and, going into the bunkhouse, swabbed some medicine over them and wrapped them up in clean strips of shirt he got out of his warbag.

Murgatroyd was asleep on one of the bunks. Stroud wondered if he ought to wake him and decided against it. Pulling off his boots and unloosening his belt, he took off his cartridge belt with its holstered pistol and wearily let himself into his bunk.

But, tired as he was, his mind kept hammering away. Had Murgatroyd found Loosh or got some inkling of his whereabouts? Where was Beulah May's father? Funny he hadn't seen the buggy in town. And funny, too, when you came right down to it, that Beulah May hadn't said anything about his disheveled appearance and the rags tied around him which she could have seen mighty easy through the rents in his brush-clawed shirt. Most women, he thought, would have made quite a fuss about seeing a man so peculiarly garbed.

Queer, the kind of things a man's mind will dredge up—like him thinking last night Chuck Murgatroyd might be working for the Pinkertons. And he might be; but sometime in his past the man had run from something and the scar of that running had become an open wound whose malignant roots twisted every thought and action. He might be a drifting gunslick but he had once been educated for something very different and Stroud wished to hell he knew what stakes the guy was playing for.

The same went for Wafer.

Stirrup's boss had shown himself to be both vulnerable and nervous. Nothing but fear could so fully account for him squandering the hold he had over Loosh in such an obvious attempt to get Stroud off Three Sixes. And the determination with which Stirrup's hands had gone after him in that Boxed Circle fracas was proof sufficient of Wafer's enmity. Wafer must have put a bounty on his scalp.

But why?

Stroud reckoned he could name a number of reasons and, if these were the right ones, Wafer would be bound to move heaven and earth in an effort to pin down Stroud's identity. He'd leave no stone unturned and, sooner or later, he was going to find out that the Lees' new ramrod was a fugitive from justice, a lifer escaped while en route to the penitentiary.

But what was Dan Wafer really after? Control of this country or mere possession of Three Sixes? That there was some connection between the boss of Stirrup and

Slade McClannigan seemed a pretty safe bet. Those sheepmen had heard about Wafer, all right. And from their talk it was a cinch they were working for McClannigan, which made it look mighty likely that Douglas had been right in assuming McClannigan was up here.

His ruse with the sheepmen had come off better than he'd hoped, but Stroud wasn't kidding himself he would have them fooled for long. At the most he would be gaining but a handful of hours and he might not gain more than that many minutes. Cheyenne Smith had heard a lot of owls hoot and would undoubtedly look into Stroud's yarn with some care before making major changes in the itinerary laid down for him. In a strange and hostile country his choice of method was limited to what he could pick up himself or what he could get from McClannigan or Wafer. He might not know Slade McClannigan was here and he may have been told to keep away from Wafer, but a twelve hour stretch of scouting should pretty well convince him the story he'd been told was sheer hot air and bullspit.

Stroud would not let himself think about Cindy—for how could he trust the resolve he had made if he kept tormenting himself with what might have been? He could not tear her image out of his heart and so he filled his head with the multitude of questions still lacking answers, and suddenly remembered something Murgatroyd had said. He was still thinking about it when he dropped off to sleep.

IT was dark when Stroud awoke, hand reaching for his gun butt. He could not guess what had pulled him from sleep and could hear no sound of breathing, but instinct told him there was someone near and he came up on one elbow, gun cocked and leveled, eyes stabbing the blackness about him.

With grim stealth he eased himself from the bunk and, barefoot, felt his way past the table. Murgatroyd's bed was cold and empty. He heard gravel grind beneath a boot and then a voice called his name from the night outside and he felt a little foolish.

It was Beulah May's voice and when he answered she said, "Cindy's back. Will you come over to the house?"

"Be over in five minutes."

He waited till she walked off, then pulled on his boots and went out to the tub and splashed water on his face. In the bunkhouse again he dug a clean shirt from his warbag and donned it, rebuckling the shell belt about his lean waist. He thrust the heavy .45 in his open-topped holster and then, picking up his hat, he stepped across the yard.

Beulah May came out of the gallery's shadows and stopped him in a band of light from the windows. She put a hand on his arm and he was shocked by the concern he saw in her face.

"Mike, something's happened to father. He hasn't come back from town and I've had no word from him. All these hours—"

"But what could have happened? Who would bother him? The road's safe enough and he hasn't any enemies—"

"How can we know that? This country's so wild and all this talk of trouble, all these cattle thefts and shooting—"

"But he's got nothing to do with that. He's probably

met some old cronies and gone off with them someplace—''

"I know. I suppose I'm foolish. But suppose this fellow, Wafer, should discover what Dad was up to?—I mean about that loan he was trying to get for Cindy. Suppose he got that loan—''

"I think you're getting yourself all upset—''

"But won't you ride to town for me and see if you can find him?''

She moved closer, her hand sliding up his arm and tightening about his elbow. "Is that too much to ask?''

He caught the fragrance of an elusive perfume, felt the pull of her worried eyes. Her husky voice, softly intimate, pleaded. "If you knew how I hate this place—how it frightens me! I would go myself but I don't know the way; and there's no one else around I could send. You will go, won't you, Mike—please? Just for me?''

Stroud, staring into those upturned eyes, wondered if she knew the front of her waist had come unbuttoned, that he could see almost all of her lush left breast in the light streaming out of the uncurtained windows. Then her arms flew up, locking hard round his neck, and the screen door opened and across her shoulder he saw the pale oval of Cindy's face.

In his mind he could not believe this was happening; it was too much the dreadful sequence of some terrible phantasmagoria. In a moment he would waken—but that was what he had thought before, that other time with. . . .

"Cindy!"

His shout ripped through the frozen quiet, tore

through the screen door's empty slamming. "Wait!" he cried. "This is not what—"

But she was already gone with a swirl of skirts, a wounded doe blindly fleeing the hunter, the sound of her passage a dying echo filtering out of that gloom-filled hall.

There was a cold constriction in the region of Stroud's stomach, a wildness surging through his brain that wanted to send him hurtling after her, dragging this damned wench with him if need be and forcing her to tell Lucinda the truth.

Then a sense of futility, of black despair, rolled over him leaving him weak and trembling, and remembered facts crushed down the urge. Better that she should hate and despise him than cry out her heart when they took him away.

Beulah May sobbed, "Mike!" and he shook himself loose with a roughness that staggered her; and felt the sting of her hand on his cheek and a bitter rage made him curse her name.

He saw the red lips smile, and a gun's blast flung him around, half falling; and the butt of his own gun rocked his palm as he snapped three shots through a whirling blackness into the diminishing echoes of a fast traveling horse.

18

NO LEG OF LAMB

STROUD did not pass out, did not quite fall down, though for three or four agonizing moments, dizzily swaying on one hand and a knee, he thought that he was going to. When his glance pulled the night into focus again Beulah May was gone, Cindy's white face was in the opening door and Chuck Murgatroyd was coming up at a lope.

"Mike!" Something was the matter with Cindy's voice. She had a hand at her throat and her eyes looked almost black in that light. "Mike—are you hurt?"

Clenching his jaws against the groan locked back of them Stroud pushed himself upright, ignoring the proffer of Murgatroyd's aid. The wicked swing of his probing stare bit into the man with a bright suspicion. "Where the—hell were you when that—gun went off?"

Murgatroyd's face was bone and skin with no expression on it.

"Any time I crack down on you," he said, "you won't be gettin' up again." He considered Stroud with that reticent look. "Do you know where that shot was fired from?"

"If I did I'd—"

"You run one bluff; better let it ride like that. The trip I took was a waste of time. No fish at the first hole. If there were any at the second they were layin' extra deep."

Stroud scowled a moment. "You see anything in town of Miz' Cindy's uncle?"

"Wouldn't know him if I saw him."

"Have you been trying to find Loosh?" Cindy asked the albino.

Murgatroyd slanched a look at Stroud and nodded. Stroud thought to see something pass between those two and distrust cut more deeply into the lines about his tight-clamped mouth.

Murgatroyd, watching, may have sensed what Stroud was thinking for he smiled a little, queerly, and said to Stroud, "Forget it. You better let Cindy look at that shoulder—"

"Cindy's going to," she said. "When you've finished, Mike, come back to the kitchen."

They heard her steps going off down the hall. "Did you get any good from your talk with the little guys?" Murgatroyd asked when the silence began to seem as though it would get uncomfortable.

"I decided you were right and didn't talk about deadlines. I got four of them to come over and help us round up a trail herd. How hard did you look for Loosh in town?"

"I went over that place with a finetoothed comb. He's not in town," Murgatroyd said with conviction. "He's been at Stirrup, an' pretty recent, but he isn't there now. You pass any words with that sheep crowd?"

Stroud told him about it and Murgatroyd said, "It could have been Smith who took that shot at you."

"He was a rotten shot whoever it was."

"I think he may have heard me. I'd been over to the cookshack feedin' my tapeworm; comin' out I happened to look over toward the house and saw you standin' there gabbin' with Cindy's cousin. You made a pretty good target in the light from those windows so, when I noticed some guy on a horse under the cottonwoods, I began to wonder what the hell he was doin' there. He was on a bay horse with a left hind leg that was white to the pastern. I couldn't see the guy's face. It come into my mind he was probably someone you knew about, someone waitin' for you. But I still didn't like the way he was sittin' in those shadows, so I cut around back of the harness shed, figuring to come up around the corner of the house where I could get a better look at him. I was halfway to the house when the guy cracked down on you an' dusted. Now was this guy Smith ridin' that kind of horse?"

Stroud shook his head. He was not too sold on Murgatroyd's story. The man might have seen such a fellow but he might also have made the whole thing up.

Then Stroud remembered the running horse. "What about the man's size? Couldn't you see what he was wearin'?"

"Hard to tell a man's size when he's on a horse. He was wearin' some kind of a long black coat; it wasn't a slicker or I'd have caught the shine. He had a black hat on his head."

"Smith was wearin' a black hat," Stroud said, and then: "Throw our hulls on a couple of horses. Bring 'em round to the door. I'll be with you in ten minutes."

Murgatroyd nodded and went off. Stroud entered the house and followed the hall to the kitchen. Cindy had water boiling on the stove and a pile of cloth for bandages waiting on the table. "Sit down in that chair and get out of that bloody shirt."

"Yes, ma'am," Stroud said meekly, and did so.

Cindy poured some salt in the water and stirred it. Then she poured half a kettleful into a basin and set it on the table to cool while she examined him. "It seems to have gone straight through," she said after a moment. "It—very luckily—doesn't seem to have struck any bone. What are these other bandages for?"

"Oh, I bumped into a couple of things," he said carelessly.

"You don't lie very well," she told him. "I guess I had better—"

"Nothing but a couple of creases. I walked into a little jam at Boxed Circle." He started to tell her Murgatroyd had pulled him out of it but, changing his mind, he said irritably, "Get this thing wrapped up if you're goin' to. I've got some more ridin' to do tonight—"

"You ought to be in a bed," she said worriedly, took a deep breath and started cleaning the wound. When it was neatly bandaged she said, "You can't wear this shirt. Leave it here. I'll wash it and—"

"I don't want you . . ." He stopped and they eyed each other uncomfortably, a vision of Beulah May rising between them.

"I've been taking care of men's clothes all my life," she said practically. Then she pulled up her chin. "Of course, if you'd rather Beulah May took care of it . . ."

"Yes," he said, "let Beulah May do it," and picked up his hat.

But at the door he turned back. "What'd you find out at Phoenix?"

Her glance turned away. She picked up the bloody rags and took the basin to the sink. Coming back she sank into a chair without speaking. Never had Stroud seen her look so bowed down; all the fine courage seemed at last to have run out of her. In a completely hopeless voice she said, "The commission house sold the note two days ago to Wafer."

STROUD came back and stood looking down at her. He dropped a hand to her shoulder and squeezed it, snatching the hand away as though burnt when he felt the involuntary contraction of her muscles.

Her eyes wouldn't look at him, stubbornly continuing to regard her folded hands. They did not see the crucified look of Stroud's face, the gone awry twist of his anguished mouth.

He didn't tell her he knew Three Sixes was doomed, that she was up against something that couldn't be licked, that he'd been through all this before. He didn't tell her it was the sheep which would beat her, that there was nothing he could do which would keep them off Three Sixes.

"Let's keep our sense of proportion," he said gently. "It's a tough break, of course, but all Wafer's gained is a piece of paper. He hasn't got the ranch and he isn't going to get it."

He left her then.

Outside, he said to Murgatroyd, "Bring the horses across the yard; I've got to get another shirt."

Afterwards, stiffly pulling himself into the saddle, he answered the other's query by saying, "It's time I looked over our range. I want to get its dimensions, but I want especially to see any rougher parts of it that have good graze."

"What you got in mind?"

"Those sheep are goin' to cross this ranch. We may as well face it. If they belong to Slade McClannigan, as I figure they do, he'll have laid down a course for his herders to follow."

"He won't have picked the roughest—"

"No. When Smith finds out I've been spinning a windy he'll come in from the south as he was probably told to do. I think McClannigan has made some kind of a deal with Wafer to insure that those sheep can get through without trouble. He's trying to show previous use so that, if this Forest bill goes through, he'll be able to get his share of the permits. Taking the sheep through Three Sixes will be Wafer's notion—another nail for the coffin, if you see what I mean."

Murgatroyd rode awhile in silence. "Seems reasonable, but I doubt they've bothered to lay out a route so far as going through this ranch is concerned. If Wafer really wants to ruin our range he'll want those sheep spread out so's to do a good job of it. He won't want them hurried through."

It was Stroud's turn at silence. "I guess you're right," he said at last. "We'll just circulate around, kind of figurin' to come up with the cut about daylight."

And that was what they did. The men had already got about a hundred head, which was evidence aplenty of how hard they had been working. Even at this early hour they were on the job and the man in charge of watching the gather told Stroud where he might locate Banjo.

They found the hunchback driving three big steers down out of the chaparral. Wiping his perspiring face Banjo told them, "Those two west tanks've gone drier'n a bone. That rain they've been catchin' to the south ain't even laid the dust up around through here. These cows an' young stuff oughta be drifted—"

"I know," Stroud nodded, "but we've got neither the men nor the time for that now. Wafer's bought up Lee's note. You can see what that means. If we don't market some beef inside the next forty days he's goin' to own this ranch without doing another thing."

Banjo swore. Murgatroyd said nothing. There was no expression on his face.

Stroud said, "How near this place is the next full tank?"

"There ain't none of 'em full an' the next nearest tank ain't no dang good at all. I—"

"What's the matter with it?"

Banjo shoved back his hat and showed a puzzled pair of eyes. "Danged if I know, now you come right down to it. Somethin' about the water—too much alkali, mebbe. Cattle won't touch it an' you can't hardly blame 'em. I was past there one day. The dang stuff stinks. Funny lookin', too."

"You know where this tank is?" Stroud asked Murgatroyd. There was a sharpness in his voice that hadn't been there before, and the albino noticed it. But he shook his head.

"It ain't hard to find," Banjo told them. "You just cut north from here an' bear a little to the east. In three-four miles you'll hit a big dang arroyo. Never mind that. Just keep on a-goin' an' 'bout a mile an' a half further you'll see a kind of a seep—ground's all discolored. Just foller that up and you'll come to the tank.''

"Let's go," Stroud said, and they set off to find it.

"What's the big idea, us huntin' a no-account tank?" grumbled Murgatroyd. "Looks like we got enough to do—"

"Maybe," Stroud said grimly, "we're goin' to find out what you're after. You and Dan Wafer and—"

Murgatroyd said, hoisting up his left leg and reaching into his boot, "I guess it's about time you had a look at these," and he handed two thin papers tightly folded across to Stroud.

"Just tell me what they are," Stroud said, not moving to touch them. "I've seen that dodge before and I'm not takin' my eyes off you."

The expression in Murgatroyd's whimsical glance was one of sardonic amusement. His lifted brows seemed rather to laugh at Stroud's dark suspicion while the eyes themselves considered him with a mingling of something which was very like respect overlaid, perhaps, with a healthy appreciation of what it might mean if he were making a mistake.

"I suggest," he smiled thinly, putting away his papers, "that neither you nor I are in this country by accident. We've found this feud makes a pretty good smoke screen—"

"I thought you didn't want Wafer to get hold of this place?"

"I *don't* want him to; but I didn't come here to risk my neck tryin' to save a doomed ranch whose entire history has been the wholesale exploitation of its neighbors. I can't work miracles and neither can you! You've already admitted we can't keep out those sheep. We couldn't keep them out if we had twice as many men—or twice that many, either. All the existing laws favor sheepmen on the open range—''

"This range ain't open."

"If you think these illegal fences—''

"Three Sixes' fences happen to be legal. They enclose patented, deeded and homesteaded land—''

"But after they've been breached and the sheep have come through, this ranch will be as ruined as the open range around it. The Lees may have a case that will stand up in court but their range won't feed cattle for another six or eight years—even if they had the price to build it up again! You can talk till hell freezes without changin' that."

Stroud's face was grim. "You better draw your time. There's no room at my wagon for a quitter, Murgatroyd."

"Oh, for— Look! I ain't quittin'. I'm just pointin' out the hopelessness of what you're tryin' to do. I'll fight hard as any man to keep Dan Wafer from takin' over this place; I don't think we can stop him but I'm game to keep on tryin'. What I'm tryin' to tell you is—''

"That you're a lawman. So what?"

"So I'd like a little help from you in case I happen to need it."

"There's the arroyo," Stroud pointed, then asked abruptly: "To what end? Or maybe you'd rather I played this blind?"

"Nope. I haven't quite figured out your game but,

whatever it is, I'm not after you—so you can take your hand away from that pistol. I'm here to hunt Lockett or find out what's become of him; and I'll say right now I think Wafer's mixed up in it.

"I think you've hit on the same notion I have—that Wafer's not after what folks think he is. Consider these facts. He's gone to considerable time and bother—not to mention expense—edgin' up on Three Sixes. Yet, if he's in with McClannigan, he knew the sheep would be comin' through here. He didn't have to buy up Lee's paper to smash this ranch; he didn't have to do it to get control of this range—a range he knew was going to be ruined for cattle."

Stroud's glance showed agreement and Murgatroyd said, "So we'll get farther faster if we pool what we know and work together."

"I'm doin' all right."

"Yeah. You're doin' great—almost rubbed out twice in twelve hours! Next time maybe you'll wind up in a box. Hasn't it struck you funny the only times this Beulah dame's dad has got off his prat long enough to go to the johnnie neither one of us fellers has been around to run into him? Where you reckon he's at now? I heard you tell that dame you didn't see him in town—but how the hell do you know you didn't? You ever got a good look at him?"

"What you gettin' at now?"

"I think he's the one took that shot at you last night."

"Cindy's *uncle?*"

"Accordin' to Banjo he wears a frock coat. I ain't heard of no one else in this country sportin' one."

"But that's plumb foolish! I been tryin' to *help* Cindy—"

"Maybe he don't want her helped—that ever strike you? And the old man up and dyin' like he done before the nap was hardly rubbed off their manners—you ever think about that? There's something wrong with that pair. Maybe you never noticed, but she lined you up like a settin' duck right in the shine of that lamplit window. You need more than help—what you need is a guardian!"

"What's all this got to do with Lockett? Or Wafer?"

"Don't slip me that. You may be greener than grass when it comes to women but on the rest of this deal you're a mile ahead of me. I saw your eyes when Banjo mentioned that tank, and I haven't forgotten one of the first things you asked me was if I'd met Lockett. You had Lockett and Wafer hooked up from the start."

"Only in the sloppiest kind of way," Stroud admitted. "Cindy told me she'd written Lockett after he'd left. Wanted to check on Craftner but got no answer. A long-time trusted foreman would have answered, so it looked pretty plain he'd never got to Tubac. Figurin' Craftner as a crook in the pay of Stirrup, and fallin' into this job so slick like he did with nothing but his word he had been tipped off by Lockett, started me wonderin' if Lockett's sudden notion to quit Three Sixes—and the strange way he seemed to disappear right after—weren't someway inspired by Mister Dan Wafer. But that's as far as I've gotten with that idea."

"What about this tank? How've you tied that in?"

"We'll know mighty quick whether it *is* tied in."

Stroud said, "There's the seep Banjo mentioned. You make anything out of it?"

They reined up and sat eying it. Murgatroyd said, "It sure stinks, all right. Funny lookin', ain't it? You'd think there'd be grass or at least some weeds around it."

Stroud said nothing but sent his horse toward the big dug tank, the rim of which showed as high ground a hundred yards to the north.

He had almost reached it when Murgatroyd, who had been leisurely coming up along the flank of the discolored seep, let out a guarded call. "Hey—wait a minute!"

That tone of suppressed excitement turned Stroud in the saddle, and he saw Murgatroyd leave his mount to squat down on his bootheels and, with the butt of his rifle, commence to prod something at the edge of the ooze.

Stroud reined his horse around and rejoined him. Sliding out of the saddle he said, "What—" and broke it off short when he saw what it was the man had prized from the seep.

It was a boot with the lower bones of a man's leg still in it.

19

POINT AND COUNTER POINT

"HOW much of that boot was showing before you—"

"Just the heel and a part of the sole."

The scalp started crawling at the back of Stroud's neck as he watched the albino fish the thing from the mire. Gingerly he lifted it out of the muck and squatted there a moment turning it around in his hands. "We've seen the last of that bird," he remarked with conviction.

"What bird?" Stroud asked.

"That shy old feller from Tonopah."

"What's Cindy's uncle got to do with that boot?"

"I don't know. Maybe nothing. But after muffin' the swell chance Beulah May gave him it's a cinch he won't be back for no encore. Now this here," he said, holding up his grisly find, "we'll label People's Exhibit A—if it ever gets to court," he added morosely.

Holding the boot by the heel with his left hand he ran the thumb of his right around the inside of the top. He found a spot he seemed to care especially for and moved his thumb, pendulum fashion, back and forth

across it with a heartiness which threatened to wear the
rotted leather through. Turning the boot then in such a
manner the protruding bones were brought within six
inches of his scrinched-up eyes, he finally grunted and
stood up.

He spat into the seep. "Rest of him's in there," he
declared with satisfaction.

"If you're talking about Lockett—"

Murgatroyd clucked. "I'm ready to look at that tank
now."

"You're guessin,' " Stroud said. "A few bones in a
boot don't—"

"Make a corpus delicti? They make one in this case.
Lockett wore a benchmade boot; this one's benchmade.
He got all his boots on order from Tony Gallardo at
Denver an' this boot's got Tony's mark. He wore a size
seven; this one's size seven. He got thrown from a
horse when he was ridin' rough string for the Lyons and
Campbell outfit an' broke his right leg just below the
knee. If you want to squint at these bones you can see
that old break. If any jury wants more than that they can
damn well come over here an' dig him out.

"My orders was to find Lockett an' I've found him.
The only thing I'm guessin' about is why he was
dumped in this seep an' who killed him. An', by the
look of your eyes when you was jawin' with Banjo, I
expect when we've looked at that tank I'll know."

"Do you?" Stroud asked when, a few moments
later, they were sitting their saddles on the raised
mound of earth which hemmed the wind-riffled surface
of the water Three Sixes' cattle wouldn't drink.

"Not yet," Murgatroyd said, looking down at it,

puzzled. "Don't remember ever seein' any water quite this color; got a kind of a shine to it, ain't it?"

Stroud nodded.

"You reckon this is what Dan Wafer's been after?"

Stroud nodded again.

"Well," Murgatroyd growled after a moment, impatiently. "Why's he want it? What's so damn important about a tank of stinkin' water?"

"It ain't the water. It's what's in it. I don't know too much about it," Stroud said grimly, "but, judgin' by what little I *do* know, I've a hunch this tank is sittin' above a hell-tearin' lake of what they call 'black gold.'"

"You mean . . . *oil?* Is that what it looks like?"

"No," Stroud said, "it's black like its name, but this rainbow colored slick is one of the pretty sure signs of its presence; and I don't think Wafer would go to all this trouble if he wasn't convinced there was a fortune under here."

But Murgatroyd was off on thoughts of his own, and he said happily, "This'll sure fix Wafer's clock. By grab, it's easy enough to figure what happened. Lockett stumbles onto the truth about this tank. Before he gets a chance to tell Lee about it, Wafer someway gets wind of what's cooking—maybe he rode up while Lockett was making some kind of tests. Anyway, he guns Lockett, dumps his carcass in that seep, goes home an' lays pipe for gettin' his hooks—"

Stroud said, "You won't pin it onto Wafer like that. In the first place you've got to remember Lockett quit Three Sixes to take a job at Tubac, accordin' to what he told Cindy's father. I'll agree to the notion this is what

Wafer's after but, if it's Lockett's remains you've found in that seep, he would have to have made this discovery *before* he quit. So what was he doin' here *after* he quit—to take a job, don't forget, at Tubac?"

Murgatroyd scowled.

"Either he stumbled onto this without realizin' its significance and wagged his jaw in front of someone who did, or he knew what he had found—"

"An' sold out to Wafer?"

"It could be like that," Stroud said thoughtfully. "But I don't believe it was. I think Lockett was on the level. I believe he said something about this tank—the queer look of this water or maybe its smell, or both—in front of someone who took it straight to Wafer, probably also not knowin'. But Wafer knew or guessed—"

"I'll subscribe to that," Murgatroyd nodded. "Some of the time Wafer was out of this country could have been spent around oil. He was over in Texas and he was on the coast, too."

"So Wafer digs up Link Craftner from somewhere, has Link spin him a story, like enough, about owning a big spread at Tubac and offering Lockett a job at a wage Lockett wasn't able to turn down. He quits Lee—"

"But how did they get him out to this tank?"

"I don't think they did," Stroud answered. "I think they killed him someplace else, then packed him out here to get rid of the body. And what better place could they hide it than—"

"What makes you think Craftner was in on this killing?"

"I've felt from the start that Craftner had a hand in Lockett's decision to go to Tubac. If Lockett didn't go to Tubac,'' Stroud explained, ''it seemed to me pretty certain that Craftner must know where he did go, because Craftner told Lee it was Lockett who'd advised him Three Sixes would be in need of a range boss. Unless Craftner knew Lockett wasn't at Tubac he would hardly have risked using Lockett's name for reference.''

''I guess you're right about that,'' Murgatroyd agreed. ''Do you reckon it was Craftner who knocked Lockett off?''

''It could have been, but I'm inclined to think it was Wafer, or someone else Wafer hired for the purpose. I don't say Craftner didn't do it, but I've got a pretty strong hunch Craftner doesn't have any idea of the true significance of this useless tank. I was tryin' to run Craftner down to have a pretty earnest talk with him when I got into that jackpot you pulled me out of. I think Craftner will crack when you put the pressure on him.''

''I'll have to look that boy up.''

Stroud nodded. ''Let's get back to the ranch. I want to see what's coming off with those sheep.''

ALL the way back to headquarters, Stroud pondered on whether or mot he should tell Cindy of their discovery. It seemed the thing to do. It was her right to know. But if he should tell her Three Sixes was probably ranching above a fortune, and it turned out that he was wrong— But he knew, deep inside him, he wasn't wrong. Stirrup's boss was too shrewd an operator to make any mistake about the value of this discovery. Ignorant punchers might never connect the appearance of that tank with oil, but Wafer was no ignorant puncher. And nothing but the conviction there was a fortune in this ground could have driven Dan Wafer. . . .

Stroud shook his head. It was the obvious answer—the only answer which would gee with the facts. There was oil on this ranch and Wafer was after it.

He must tell Cindy.

Even though it were a cruel thing to show a girl a vision of wealth within her grasp when it looked so unlikely she'd ever close her hands on it, he'd tell her. Because the pieces had all dropped into place now, all the cogs were meshing and he could see this thing to the end of its sequence. Even Cindy's uncle, 'that shy old man from Tonopah,' had assumed his rightful place. The cards were all down and the bluffing was over.

Only one thing stood between Cindy and happiness—between her and the wealth which lay concealed beneath that tank. One thing.

Wafer.

And Stroud knew how to stop Wafer. Chuck Murgatroyd had told Stroud how to do that.

THEY were in the pines now just above Three Sixes. Looking around, Stroud said, "You aimin' to take that thing to the table?"

Murgatroyd scowled. "Reckon I could make out to hide it; not much sense, I guess, upsetting those two fillies. But, damn it, this thing is evidence, Stroud—"

"You could cache it under one of these trees. Or in the branches. You could come back with a gunnysack."

"Well . . . yeah. Guess nobody'll bother it in that length of time."

THE ranch lay wrapped in the quiet of noontime. A sleepy lizard drowsed in the sun and two fat flies were rendering a duet above the leaky trough when they rode into the yard. "Expect I'd better see Cindy," Stroud said, turning his pony. Murgatroyd nodded and rode on toward the barn.

As Stroud got out of the saddle Beulah May looked up from her chair on the gallery. He would have passed with the civility he gave any woman had the girl been content to have it so.

She was not. She got up. She put her hands on her hips and thrust out her bosom. Red lips curled. "Not so fast—Cindy's busy. But if you'd care to sit down—"

"No, thanks," Stroud said, "but when he comes back you can tell Slade McClannigan—"

He broke off, head canted, startled by a sound which had come out of the house. Turned completely still, glance caught by the malice of Beulah May's frozen smile, he heard a stifled cry—the slap and scrape of scuffling bodies; and would have hurled himself forward save that, just at that moment, something cold and very hard was suddenly rammed against his spine.

"I don't think, *Mister* Stroud, I'd do a thing if I were you."

20

WAFER STRIKES

THE screen door was thrust violently open and Cindy, with a gag in her mouth and arms lashed behind her, was pushed roughly onto the gallery by a big bearded man with crossed gun belts who grinned hugely at the look he saw in Stroud's eyes.

Another bearded man came around the corner of the house leading five saddled horses.

"Hey, Ben!" someone called from the direction of the barn. "What you want we should do with this one?"

"Fetch him over an' bring his horse," the man behind Stroud said; and then, to the girl: "Grab his gun, Miss."

With smiling venom Beulah May jerked the pistol from its holster. She smashed Stroud across the face with it twice and then stepped back, breathing heavily.

Cindy's eyes were stark.

Stroud, with the blood dripping down his torn cheeks, met her look and quietly smiled.

Ben Redcliff, stepping around him, said, "You're

goin' to need that grin. You had fair warnin', bucko—I told you to get out of this country.''

He snapped a look at the man beside Cindy. ''Get that gag off her, Lem. She can't bother us now; let her yap if she wants to.''

The man pulled the dirty neckerchief loose. Cindy flung the sheriff a withering look. ''Just what do you think you're doing here, Ben?''

''Still playin' it high an' mighty, eh?'' There was a jubilant note in Redcliff's voice. ''Wait'll the papers get hold of this story! 'Rustler Queen—' ''

''Answer my question!''

A malevolent sneer twisted Redcliff's mouth. ''I been keepin' my finger on the pulse of the voters. There's a bunch of 'em hollerin' for some law around here. They're plumb tired of seein' you Lees cuttin' fences, runnin' off cattle— Say! Where's your ol' man?''

She tossed the hair back out of her face. ''My father is dead.''

Redcliff's eyes slimmed to slits. He spat and said harshly, ''He sure picked a good time.''

Two men came up with their guns prodding Murgatroyd. ''Ain't nobody else on the place—''

''All right. Tie his arms back of him, set him on his horse an' put a wrap around his ankles—an' make damn sure he don't get away from you. The rest of 'em's prob'ly off hidin' them cattle. When you get done, tie up Stroud the same way.''

Cindy's cheeks were white but her voice blazed with anger. It almost seemed for a moment old Cyrano stood there. ''I want an answer from—''

''You've got your answer! I'm breakin' up a nest of

cow thiefs an' riddin' this country of a bushwhackin' killer! Is that plain enough for you?''

"It's a lie!'' Cindy cried.

Redcliff looked at his men and laughed. Answering grins flickered across several faces. Redcliff's gangling shape wheeled round. "A lie, eh? You'll have a pretty hard time, missy, gettin' these boys to swaller that slop after what they've seen with their own naked eyes.''

He gave her a bland, slyly mocking look the while he declared indignantly for all who might hear, "I've had my suspicions of that brother of yours for a considerable while, but he never had the guts to come right out in the open with his stealin' till you hired this killer, Stroud, to back his hand—''

"Mike Stroud isn't a killer!''

The sheriff smiled smugly. "It'll take more'n the word of a rustler's queen to make this country believe that now.'' Without taking his look off the girl, he said: "Stroud, I'm arrestin' you—''

"You can't!'' Cindy screamed, and would have run to his side if the bearded deputy had not reached out and grabbed her. "You *can't!*'' she sobbed. "You—''

"I can, will and *am,*'' Redcliff said, plainly exulting in the sight of her tears.

"He has a right to know why you're arresting him. Tell him and give him his chance—''

"I aim to. The same kinda chance he give them Boxed Circle boys. I'm arrestin' him for murder, an' this other one for rustlin'. Your outfit, led by Loosh Lee an' this Stroud, pulled a raid on Stirrup two nights ago. They got a big batch of cows an' was rushin' them east for the mountains when they run into trouble at the Boxed Circle line camp just above your fence. Must of been quite an occasion; but your bunch got away with—''

"I don't believe it!"

The bearded man who had hold of her said, ''We all seen the corpses. We spent most of the night packin' them in to the coroner.''

"Five of 'em," Redcliff smiled with relish, grimly ticking them off on his fingers. ''Loosh Lee, Link Craftner an' three boys from Boxed Circle. Deader than doornails.''

Stroud thought Cindy would fall. Her eyes were like holes burned in a bed sheet. ''How can you know that?'' she whispered. ''How can you know that's what happened?''

"Hell, the ground's all run over with cow tracks," Lem growled.

"An'," Redcliff said, "we've got Craftner's sworn statement; his dyin' testament made before witnesses. One of Wafer's crew cut the sign of that herd an' like to wore a horse out gettin' to Stirrup with the news. Wafer took ten men an' cut for the hills. They never come up with the stolen cattle but they heard the gunshots an' rode for Boxed Circle. Time they got to the line camp the fightin' was over, but this guy Craftner was still alive.'' He said vindictively to Stroud, ''You'll have a hell of a time gettin' round the dyin' word of one of your own outfit!''

Murgatroyd asked, ''What did Craftner say?''

"He admitted Three Sixes had run off with them cows. Said he'd been against this stealin' right from the start, but that Loosh an' his ol' man wouldn't listen; then, after the girl come home with this killer, they said he wasn't to be range boss no more an' give the job to

Stroud. Said Stroud was willin' to do like they wanted an' helped them cook up this raid on Stirrup. Then, when they was surprised by the boys from Boxed Circle, Stroud give orders to wipe 'em out an' started the ball rollin' by droppin' Tularosa. Craftner started to put in a protest. Loosh whirled round an' knocked him outa the saddle, shootin' him as he fell. That's all we got out of him but it's all any jury in this country would ask for—an' all ten of them punchers heard him tell it!''

Cindy's stare went off focus. She swayed and would have fallen if the bearded Lem hadn't caught her.

Stroud stood like a graven image, the eyes looking out of his battered face showing no more expression than two pieces of stone.

Redcliff said, "Ease her down on the floor an' untie her. She'll come round in a minute. We got no time for swoonin' females; this girl can look after her."

Beulah May said self-righteously, "I'm leaving. If you think I'd be willing to stay around here after—"

"Go where you like but don't get in my way," the sheriff said testily; and, to the others, "Couple of you get Stroud up on a horse, an' watch him. Watch both of 'em, but don't take your eyes off Stroud for a minute. Don't take any chances. Shoot first an' give me your version of it later. I'll be seein' you boys in town. Shake a leg now."

21

DEAD OR ALIVE!

REDCLIFF had been right to warn his men never to take their eyes off Stroud. Three Sixes' range boss, riding between two burly deputies in the van of this silent cavalcade, had reached that point of desperation where only the sheriff's grim instructions were keeping him from attempting the utterly impossible.

Four guards, two prisoners.

But he knew the actual odds were much greater for the guards were armed, their movements unhampered. They'd been plainly invited to shoot on suspicion. With arms lashed behind them and ankles tied beneath the bellies of their horses, there was nothing that he or Murgatroyd could do short of courting instant death.

And Murgatroyd's stake in this affair did not call for heroic measures. It hardly went beyond the fate of a job which was not greatly threatened in any event. For if it were Redcliff's intention to work up a mob into hanging them both on Craftner's evidence as relayed by Wafer, he would not dare let such end come to Murgatroyd once the man had shown him those papers.

For himself Stroud cared nothing. Death from a bullet held little terror for a man who'd been sentenced to Yuma for life. He would as soon die that way as rot in a jail or kicking his breath out at the end of a rope. It was for *Cindy* that Stroud was desperate.

He had had no chance to see her alone, to tell her the truth of what Wafer was after. With that knowledge, properly shared, she might yet have secured sufficient backing from capital to have nullified everything Wafer had done. It would not have fetched back her brother but, with money behind her, she might have pinned Loosh's death—or the responsibility for it—on Wafer. Now, not knowing these things and with Stroud the prisoner of a vindictive sheriff whom Cindy herself had publicly scorned, she would be stripped of everything—perhaps even of honor.

He simply *had* to get loose.

Yet of what avail would his escape be to Cindy if he were shot down before he could reach her? Being hanged or shot for killing Dan Wafer was one thing. Being killed vainly trying to get clear of this posse was something else again and could do her no good whatever. Yet this was the thing he always came back to. With time running out he devised and discarded wild plan after plan only to be brought inevitably face to face with the knowledge that no man was faster than a powder-sped bullet.

And she needed him *now*. Not tomorrow or the next day when, crushed by the deaths of her father and brother, remorselessly hounded by the minions of Stirrup, her ranch overrun by McClannigan's sheep and ruined for cattle beyond hope of repair, with no hope left she might sell out for any crust Wafer cared to throw to her.

The thought was maddening. And McClannigan! God, what a fool he had been not to have given more thought to that counterfeit uncle. And memory had warned him that very first night when he'd sat in the rain looking after that buggy. He had thought at the time there had been something familiar about that man's voice. Yet on he had gone, blinded by his own wrongs at the hands of this man's brother, piling folly onto folly, doing nothing toward the accomplishment of the task which had brought him into these hills— doing nothing actually which was of any use to Cindy. She would have been better off had he never set foot on Three Sixes at all.

It was Murgatroyd who had jogged him awake to the true identity of Cindy's supposed uncle. And yet this business of windows was something Stroud should have thought about. The other time they'd been curtained with the light shining bright behind them.

Stroud looked up at the sun. He had no means of knowing how far they had come, but they were still in the hills. Tied as he was, and with his spurs taken off before these possemen had put him in the saddle, he wasn't even sure he could get this horse to running; it was the grulla he'd been riding most of the night and all this morning. He doubted if there was much run left in him; and the whiskered Lem had hold of the reins and the man on the other side rode with a cocked rifle leveled at Stroud across the pommel of his saddle. It might be wiser, he thought, to go on into town and try to make his break there in the confusion of their arrival.

But had he any guarantee he'd get to town? Where was Redcliff? Why had he left them? Had he gone to meet Wafer to report Stroud's arrest? Supposing the man had finally tied up with Stirrup—would Wafer care to risk the chance of having Stroud faced with a jury of cowmen? Wasn't it much more likely that Redcliff, or another of Wafer's understrappers, was waiting even now somewhere ahead along this trail to stop Stroud's mouth with a burst from a rifle?

Again Stroud's mind went over the chances. They were practically non-existent. No amount of wishful thinking could change this. But there was a curve up ahead about a thousand feet where the trail swung around the blind side of a butte, dropping sharply thereafter as best he remembered in a loop to the river. Perhaps for some part of a second then, while these newly made deputies—as almost any man would—let their eyes play over the valley floor, he would have the best chance he could look for.

He would have to take it.

He did not glance toward the pair riding one on either side of him, even covertly, for should they happen to notice him doing so they might think it peculiar and become suspicious. Neither did he pretend to grow sleepy nor groggy for he had done no spadework toward this presumption and to do so now might but serve to increase the guards' vigilance.

His mind, razor sharp as in most times of crisis, warned him to do nothing which might even remotely tend to attract their notice; nor was he forgetting the pair behind him for, although their prime concern was for Murgatroyd, these too might take instant alarm were he in any way to deviate from riding habits already displayed.

He was, in fact, become acutely self-conscious and had to force himself to uncock tensed muscles lest even so little as a too-still back or a too stiffly held neck unwittingly give the show away. He was preparing to gamble with Cindy's whole future, a thing to him far more precious than life.

Despite every exertion of will, however, the nearer they came to the bend in the trail the more tightly Stroud's anxious muscles contracted. They were like coiled springs when the shadow of the butte fell across the grulla's path.

The start of the bend was twenty strides away when the bearded Lem dropped Stroud's reins across his lap and, with a leisurely yawn, fished out Durham and papers. Stroud almost cursed with the irony of it. He was mightily tempted to try his luck anyway but common sense weaned him away from the impulse.

He watched Lem's shadow roll a smoke left-handed and could feel sweat standing on his back like drops of water as he counted the baldfaced grulla's steps and wondered if Lem were going to take long enough. . . .

Lem wasn't.

With twelve strides to go the man's hand ran a match across his chaps, fetching it to a stop with the lighted end against his quirley. With ten still to go he broke the match and dropped it. There were eight still remaining when the guard on Stroud's left growled, "How about givin' me a crack at those makin's?"

With six strides left Lem said, "To hell with you. I hev to work for what *I* git."

The curve's blind beginning was just beyond the grulla's nose when Stroud in a voice that creaked like a gate hinge gruffly muttered, "Sack in my right shirt pocket if you want it," and almost quit breathing as, with his rifle's snout gone completely off focus, the man leaned across him to get at the bait.

With a scream bloodcurdling as a Comanche Indian's, Stroud squeezed the grulla's barrel with both knees. The terrified gelding took to air like a rocket, jouncing the tobacco-hunting deputy loose and driving both heels into the flank of Lem's pony which, with a squeal of rage, promptly ducked its head and put its hind end above it. The cursing Lem, with left hand darting after Stroud's departing reins and right hand trying to yank a belt gun from its holster, was caught off balance and parted from his saddle like a catapulted rock.

A rifle banged from someplace behind them and Stroud's bolting grulla, careening around the butte on two legs, was gathering himself for a frantic run when a white-faced Cindy wildly waving a pistol moved out of the brush on her big black horse.

"Don't head him!" Stroud cried, having visions of a pile-up. "He won't run far—swing your horse alongside an' ride him out!"

They flashed past the girl like a runaway express and then, on her fresher mount, she was up with them, the black and the grulla running neck and neck.

"Crowd him into the brush!" Stroud shouted and, half a minute later, she had the grulla stopped.

"Quick—" Stroud grunted, "cut my arms loose! We've got to save Chuck, an' those deputies are—"

"They can't see us here—"

"But they'll be here in a minute!"

"If this thing were only sharper," Cindy muttered, feverishly sawing at his ropes with her dull-bladed hunting knife. "I—"

With an effort that turned his battered face nearly purple Stroud's straining biceps parted the half cut strands just as the first cursing posseman came larruping around the bulge of the butte. Ignoring his still-tied ankles, Stroud snatched the rifle from Cindy's scabbard, slammed the butt to his shoulder and squeezed the trigger.

The deputy's horse went end over end, bringing up in the brush with its neck twisted under it. The deputy, flung clear, lay in the trail without movement. But Stroud knew the others would soon be along. Holding the 1 fle ready, his narrowed eyes watched the trail while Cindy, down off her black, frantically hacked at the ropes which imprisoned his ankles—and suddenly they were free. Stroud grimaced in pain as blood rushed through his numbed legs.

Cindy pulled herself back into the saddle. "Mike—"

"C'mon! We've got to get—"

A slug, droning through the brush like a hornet, slammed into the butte and went tearing off in shrill ricochet. Stroud, swearing, left the saddle, almost falling as his feet struck earth. He jerked Cindy roughly from hers, pulling her down below the wind-tossed tops of the chaparral.

He could feel her heart beating wildly against him. Her harried eyes, too wide, were dark with alarm. "They've cut around—"

"Cut around nothin'! I've been lookin' for this,"

Stroud said harshly. "That's Redcliff, damn him—he was holed up below someplace waitin' for a shot at us!"

"If we could work through this brush—"

"Too thick," Stroud scowled. "We'd make too much noise. Look—you've got to get out of this. If they can't smoke me out any other way they'll be firin' this brush. Listen! There's oil on your place—probably worth a fortune. It's what Wafer's after. If I don't get clear of this mess, you go to Jeff Douglas, tell him about it. He's a square-shooter an' he'll know what's best for you—got that?"

Her eyes clung to his face. She put a hand on his shoulder. She passed the tips of her fingers over his cheekbones, over his throbbing temples. "You're just thinking of . . . me?"

"I'm thinkin' about your happiness, Cindy—about these lyin', cheatin', cowardly polecats that would take that oil away from you! Don't let them! If anything happens to me you go to Jeff Douglas—right away. You'll remember that, won't you?"

"But . . . but I don't want anything to happen to you. Mike! Oh— Mike . . .!"

He whirled away from her, shaking. With raised voice he cried: "Redcliff! Can you hear me?"

"I hear you."

"Lucinda Lee's in here with me. I want you to let her out of this."

"Be glad to, Stroud. Just throw down your guns an' come—"

"I'm talkin' about Cindy!"

"So am I. She stays right where she is till you throw down—"

"You would do that? Good Lord, man! With bullets—"

"Save your breath," Redcliff sneered. "If it bothers you what might happen to her, come out of there now with your hands up."

Stroud knuckled the burning sweat from his eyes. "All right," he said, "I'll—"

"No!" Cindy cried, and clung to him, trembling. "Do you think I would care what happened to me if they killed you? That's what they mean to do—you know it is, Mike! Don't let them take you! Don't ever leave me. . . ."

She was crying with face pressed against his chest, sobbing as women do when they're hurt. "Merciful Christ!" Stroud breathed, and stood there like a man turned to stone.

"Well!" Redcliff snarled. "Are you comin' or ain't you?"

Cindy pulled herself away from Stroud. "No!" She whirled toward the sound of Redcliff's voice and cried: "No—I won't let him! If you're going to kill him you can kill me, too!"

"Well, if that's the way you want it. You heard her, boys. If she chooses to side a rustler caught red-handed there ain't nothin', I guess, the law can do about it. Start riddlin' that brush."

Stroud yanked Cindy down flat against the rough ground. And none too soon, for that murderous salvo clipped twigs from the brush all about them. Stroud's baldfaced grulla dropped in its tracks like a poleaxed steer and the girl's big black, with reins flying, took off through the growth with a terrified squeal.

Redcliff's voice through the fading uproar called:

"Last chance, Stroud. If you don't want that girl shot to doll rags, come outa there pronto!"

But the girl wouldn't have it. She clung to Stroud with fingers of steel. "If you go they might as well kill me too. I'll have nothing to live for . . . don't you know that, Mike?"

Stroud moaned through locked lips in the agony of knowledge. He could see his reflection in the depths of her eyes and in unbearable anguish he cried, "When he called me a killer back there in your yard he spoke no more than the truth. I was convicted of killing a sheep-man, Angus McClannigan. Murder, they called it—"

But she covered his mouth with her fingers. "Do you think that could make any difference?"

"But, Cindy—I was sentenced to Yuma *for life!*"

"Hush. Look—" she said, pointing, "there's a way through the brush—the way Blackie went. Hurry!"

"You comin' outa there, Stroud?"

That was Redcliff again, but the girl shook her head. Fiercely holding his arm she pulled him into the path her black horse had made.

"All right, boys," the sheriff said, "close in. I want that man, dead or alive."

22

ROCK BOTTOM

RIDING double, it was full dark when they reached the Boxed Circle line camp, the one place, Stroud said, where neither Redcliff nor Wafer would think of looking. For what seemed like hours they had played hide and seek through the brush with that kill-crazy posse, had been all but washed up when Stroud, carrying the girl, had finally stumbled onto her horse with its reins snagged fast in a thicket of catclaw. The horse was all that had saved them.

Getting down before the shack, Stroud put up his arms to help Cindy but she said, "I'm all right now," and got down by herself though her scratched cheeks were drawn with weariness. "We need rest but I think we ought to push on, Mike. We ought to put all the distance—"

"No," Stroud said. "You're forgetting the oil. We can't let—"

"Don't you understand yet? Can I say it any plainer? That oil, the ranch, means nothing without you. I don't care if we don't have *anything*."

In the dark Stroud stood without movement. He told

her gently again he was a fugitive from justice, a convicted murderer, sentenced to life imprisonment at Yuma. "I have no future, nothing to offer you or any woman—"

"It's you I want, Mike. You're all the future I'd ask."

Stroud groaned. "Look," he cried, and told her how Douglas had turned him loose, what it was the Chief Forester had wanted him to do.

"You'll have to do it then, Mike. He's depending on you."

"But can't you see that when it's done they'll send me back to prison? *For life!*" he said bitterly. "If I tried to run—and I'll admit I've thought about it—if I actually got clear it would be just like he said, every man's hand against me. You can't live like that. I'd be on the dodge, a hunted convict till someone dropped me or the doors of Yuma Prison—"

"Tell me, did you kill this man, this McClannigan?"

When he didn't answer she said without censure, "There was a girl?"

He nodded.

"Would it help if you told me about it?"

"We were engaged to be married. She was the daughter of a well-to-do cowman. We were having a little trouble with sheep about then; McClannigan's crowd was after our range. I got a note from the girl after supper one evening asking me to meet her at a cabin out of town.

"There was a light behind the drawn curtains. I walked into the place at the appointed time. The girl was there, naked on the bed in the arms of this sheepman. There was no question of forcing. The girl was enjoying herself.

"That same night McClannigan was killed. He was found with his throat cut, tangled in those sheets. My knife was found with him, covered with blood. I'd been seen going into the cabin. The witness who saw me was a man of integrity, our local sheriff, who had also been summoned to the place by a note. Another witness, one of the dead man's crew, swore he'd heard me threaten to kill Angus McClannigan if one of his sheep put foot on my land. His sheep were all over it. The jury gave its verdict without leaving the box."

"But you didn't kill him?"

"What could that have helped? My pride? I had none; all I wanted was to get away someplace. And that was the final argument, the one that told most against me. I was picked up forty miles from the place, plainly bent on quitting the country."

"And the girl's own evidence? She accused—"

"God above! The girl was never brought into it."

"Not . . . ?" She stared at him with a shocked surprise. "You mean neither you nor this so-honest sheriff could bear—"

"Bearing had nothing to do with it. The sheriff was advised, in a note signed 'well wisher,' merely to be around there at the specified time. He was not told to enter the cabin; the place was being lived in and the owner—a friend of mine—was able to prove later he'd been twenty miles away. I doubt if Sheriff Rhodes ever suspected a girl was in there—certainly not *that* girl. Why should he? Would you expect the daughter of the county's leading cowman to have anything in common with a bullypuss sheep boss?"

"And you never told? Mike, she wasn't worth—"

"You don't get it," he said, shaking his head wearily. "It wasn't what *I* thought about the girl; it was what others believed . . . the upstanding, right minded folks in that country. There was no evidence she had been there. It was just getting dark when the sheriff saw McClannigan go into the cabin, pull down the shades and put on a lamp. Perhaps a quarter hour later he saw me ride up and go in—says he recognized me plainly in the light of the opening door. After he saw me come out he went back to town, thinking that someone had been pulling his leg. When the body was discovered he remembered I had 'looked kind of funny'—"

"But you *didn't* kill him, did you?"

"No, Lucinda, I didn't kill him. But never in a hundred years could I—"

"The girl must have killed him."

"But why? They were lovers—"

"Lovers have quarreled before this, Mike. She may—"

"Speculation's no good. I've been over this thing—"

"She sent you the note."

"I don't know." Stroud said irritably, "I've asked myself that a thousand times and I still don't know. It looked like her writing, her signature. But why would she want me to see a thing like that? She *wanted* to be in that feller's arms! I've wondered if her father could some way have stumbled onto—"

"But would he have left your knife there? Would he have sent you that note?"

Stroud shook his head drearily. "No. He was my friend."

Cindy gripped his arm tightly. "I think that girl deliberately—"

"I still can't believe it. And don't forget, the sheriff also was invited—"

"But not asked inside! Mike, be reasonable! You know very well you were deliberately lured there to be charged with that man's murder. If the girl didn't kill him herself she could hardly fail to know who did. This is no time to think of her folks, her reputation. We've got to make her tell!"

Stroud's laugh was bitter. "The girl is dead."

Cindy went back a step, eyes staring at him fixedly. "Oh, no, Mike— *No!*"

"They told me about it while I was waiting for the marshal to take me to Yuma. Her neck was broken. She was thrown from a horse."

In the shack behind them a floorboard groaned. Stroud spun like a cat. A gun gleamed in his hand. *"Come out of there–careful."*

The dim outline of a man with hands stretched above his head took shape in the black rectangle of the door.

"I'm mighty glad," that man drawled, "I've never felt called on to tackle you, Stroud. With a draw like that you'd probably turned me into a colander."

"You've got some damned unhealthy habits, friend."

"Hell—I've been asleep in there. Could I help it if you came here with your gab an' woke me up?"

"How'd you get away from that posse? How'd you know we'd come here?"

"I didn't know," Murgatroyd growled, and then, gruffly: "You may as well know I heard what you said."

"What are you figurin' to do about it?"

"Do? Nothing. None of my business—"

"You're a lawman, ain't you?"

"You think every range dick is a goddam scalp-hunter?"

Some of the coiled spring look went out of Stroud's shoulders. He put his gun away. "Sorry, Chuck. You get to thinkin' that way after awhile." Jeff Douglas knew. *Every man's hand against you*, Jeff had said. "How'd you get loose?"

"I didn't have much trouble after you let out that yell. I'd been figurin' you'd start somethin' an' kept my eye peeled. When you dived for that bend the whole outfit went to pieces; the pair watchin' me plumb forgot me entirely. They lit out after you like flies after sorghum. I just cut for the brush an' kept goin'. One of 'em drove a shot in my direction but I was damn near out of range when he done it an' he never even bothered to turn his horse.

"I went to the shack of a nester I knew. After he'd looked at my papers he cut me loose. I ducked back to the ranch, aimin' to get that roundup crew. Wafer'd beat me to it. That beef is scattered hell west an' crooked. Not a sign of those squatters. Only ones I could find was Banjo an' Charlie an' they've et their last meals. Wafer made a clean sweep—nothin' left of the buildings but a heap of hot ashes. Three Sixes is done as a cow spread. Those sheep are crossin' the river right now."

Stroud sighed. He said bitterly, "Wafer an' Redcliff have come to terms." He stared down at his hands, tired shoulders sagging. "I had reckoned to hold those sheep back awhile by blastin' Stirrup's dam and raising the level of the river, but I suppose it's too late for that now."

"By this time the bulk of them will be across They're probably damn near onto our wire." There was regret in Murgatroyd's voice, and conviction. "Stroud, we're licked. We ain't got a dog's chance of savin' that spread. We've got no men, no money an' no damn time. Wafer'll have his crew out scourin' the hills. What the hell are you waitin' around for? You heard Miz' Cindy. You know how she feels. Don't be a fool, man—take her! Take her an' dig for the tules!"

23

LONG PASS

"NO."

"You've got everything to gain an' not a—"

"Runnin's no answer," Stroud said doggedly.

"What's the matter with you, boy? Runnin's better than rottin' at Yuma! You better be thinkin' about Miz Cindy—"

"I'm thinkin' about her. That's why I ain't runnin'. What kind of a life would that be for a woman?"

"Maybe you'd rather have her watch you kickin' your life out at the end of a rope?" He glowered. "What the hell can you do you ain't already tried?"

"There's a way to stop Wafer—remember?"

Murgatroyd's stare was sharp in the shadows. He half opened his mouth and then, abruptly, shut it. Neither of them looked at the white-cheeked girl.

Stroud said, "See if you can scare me up a fresh horse."

Cindy caught at his arm. "Mike . . . you're not going to leave me?"

"Only for a awhile," he said gruffly. "I've remembered something. I want to look at those sheep."

Murgatroyd went into the shack and came back with his saddle. "About that killin'," he said to Stroud. "You ever think who stood to make the most profit?"

"Any cowman in that country might have profited by it. The sheep threatened all of us."

The albino eyed him a moment, shifted the saddle to his other shoulder. "You two better try an' get some rest."

"Get me a mount too, Chuck," Cindy called after him.

He was back in an hour with three fresh horses. He saddled them while Stroud tried to persuade Cindy into remaining where she was. But she refused to listen. "I'm going with you."

Discontent rippled Stroud's gaunt cheeks but he quit arguing. He said: "I think I've got this deal doped out. The coming of these sheep, in the first place, had nothin' to do with Three Sixes. Ruinin' this range was a brainstorm of Wafer's intended to knock down the worth of this land. These sheep, I believe, belong to Slade McClannigan. If McClannigan doesn't own them, he's back of them. His intention has been to use these sheep—even sacrificing them if he has to—to establish prior use of at least a portion of the range which will comprise the Crook National Forest if the present bill goes through. Only by establishin' a prior use will he stand any chance of getting grazing permits later. With the last of the open range about gone he's got to get those permits, drastically reduce the size of his flocks or go out of the business. So they're goin' to push these sheep through fast as they can. What's the quickest way they can get there?"

Cindy said, "Through Long Pass."

Looking up, Murgatroyd rubbed the bunched reins against his cheek. "You figurin' to stop 'em?"

"I'm goin' to try. One of the things Jeff Douglas didn't tell me was to keep sheep out of that region. He couldn't afford to, but the main concern of this new Forest bill is conservation, protection of the watershed. You know what sheep will do."

He said to Cindy: "Moon will be up inside a couple hours. I want to be on high ground overlookin' that pass when it gets up."

HE was.

A rough place, that gorge between the peaks. Sheep wouldn't find it easy going. They'd have to hack their way through horse-high chaparral before they could reach the northern slope. The ground over there was bare, a black stretch of malpais composed of up-and-down slants whose sheer surfaces were gouged and broken up by countless gullies which came together in the round bowl of a valley, afterwards dropping in dizzying descent into the cliff-rimmed bottom of a narrow box canyon. It was this middle fork down which Cheyenne Smith and his sheep would have to come, and Stroud's look showed satisfaction as he eyed it.

Murgatroyd said, "Too far to drop rocks."

Stroud said to Cindy, "Where's the nearest place that we can get a bunch of horses?"

Cindy said straightaway, "There's a band of wild broncs—maybe forty or fifty—in a mountain meadow back of Allfritch's Knob—you know the place, Chuck. Down below, where the valley opens up above Long Pass, there's a bunch of Three Sixes saddle stock grazing—or was. Of course, Wafer—"

"Chuck," Stroud said, pointing, "can you bring the broncs Cindy mentioned down onto that flat an' ease them into that holdin' pen?"

"Can try."

"Tryin' ain't good enough. I want those broncs put into that pen. I want them there by mid-mornin' in market condition. Get at it."

He sat a long while thinking after the last sound of Murgatroyd's travel had faded. Finally he said, "You reckon we could talk a few of the small owners into givin' us a hand? I just want them to ride across that slope down there."

But Cindy shook her head.

Stroud told her then about his talk with the sheepmen. "I was thinkin' maybe we could sell Smith the notion it was Randymier's bunch. Probably Wafer'll have told him by now there ain't no Randymier, but he can't know Wafer much better'n he knows me. If a bunch of riders happened to skyline themselves where he could get a quick look at them he might make the wrong guess an' play right into our hands."

Cindy sighed. "I'm afraid Chuck has the right of it. You've done everything you can—we all have, and it's just no use."

Stroud got up and moved around a little, studying the rough ground below with grim care. At last he turned, came back and faced her.

Moonlight showed the deep-etched lines which weariness, pain, despair and anger had graven into those battered features, the hunted sharpness of narrowed stare.

"Murgatroyd reckons we've reached the end of our rope. I ain't admittin' it. We've spent too much time tryin' to beat a stacked deck; lookin' at Wafer from the wrong end of the glass. He's played his cards well but he wasn't the dealer and the chips came out of another man's pocket—a fact I've just realized. Havin' Wafer in front of us I made the same mistake you did, figurin' him the brass-collar dog in this deal. Yet you'd told me the truth. He was nothing but a bum—till McClannigan backed him."

"You mean the brother of the man you were convicted of killing?"

"Yeah," Stroud nodded—"the killin' that wouldn't focus. Again I was too close. I was jest the feller at the short end of the stick and all I could think of was that I'd been framed. I couldn't remember anyone who would hate me that bad an' I couldn't think why the girl should have helped him. She didn't of course—not intentionally. The killer, soon's he found she was secretly playin' house with Angus, simply recognized the perfect solution to his problem an' took advantage of it. I didn't have any secret enemy. I wasn't standin' in anyone's way. Angus was the man that trap was rigged for. He was killed by his brother, Slade McClannigan."

"Mike!" Cindy cried, and jumped up and caught hold of him. "Can you prove it?"

"I reckon not," Stroud said. "But all the pieces fit. Slade's a power in this country—all over the West; more irons in the fire than a man has fingers. Why share the fruits of his schemin' with a quarrelsome, belligerent roughneck brother when Smith could do the same work an' for a quarter of Angus' take? No, I can't prove it, his tracks are too well covered. But I'm convinced in my own mind. The guy back of all this stuff is Slade McClannigan.''

''But if you knew all this—''

''I didn't know it. I've only just now doped it out. Up till this mornin' I'd no idea where to look for McClannigan. I never guessed he was hidin' right under my nose! He's the feller that's been posin' as your long lost uncle—''

Cindy stared. ''Talbot *Lee?*''

''Douglas told me the man was a born actor,'' Stroud nodded. ''I reckon he must have got quite a turn when he woke up that morning an' found you had Mike Stroud on your payroll—''

''Dad's death!'' Cindy whirled. ''Do you suppose . . . ?''

''It wouldn't surprise me. Him or that fancy baggage he's got with him. I'm bettin' she's no more his daughter than I am.''

He studied the valley spread below them again, estimating its probable radius as something under two miles, paying particular attention to the way its north quarter funneled into Long Pass. The Three Sixes saddle stock Cindy had mentioned was near the valley's south entrance, contentedly grazing the lower slopes of the mountainside which formed its west rim. These horses weren't more than a scant half mile from the holding pen, separated from it by what looked like brush but was probably a heavy stand of scrub oak.

As near as he could judge the holding pen couldn't be seen from either the west or east slopes and was certain to be hidden from anyone entering the valley from the south, which was the way Cheyenne Smith would have to bring in the sheep.

As though reading his thoughts Cindy said abruptly, "Smith's bunch are going to see that saddle stock. What if they decide to borrow or steal them?"

"It's a chance we've got to take. I don't think they'll bother. I'm countin' strong he hasn't got hold of McClannigan an' stronger still he doesn't wholly trust Wafer. There's no honor among crooks. It's a dog-eat-dog business and I think Smith's smart enough to keep his eyes peeled. No matter what Wafer's told him I'm bettin' brother Randymier's still in his mind."

"You think he'll be looking for trouble?"

"Put yourself in his place. Smith's heard the owl hoot. I don't believe he's a guy that would trust his own grandmother."

Stroud studied the scene spread below a while longer. "We ain't lost the ranch yet—at least you've still got title. But we can't go back. So we strike where we can. We hit McClannigan's sheep."

Cindy's tone held alarm. "You mean . . . just you and me and Chuck Murgatroyd?"

"It's the only thing I know to do. They won't be expectin' it—Wafer an' Slade won't. After that raid Stirrup made they probably figure we're splittin' the breeze. Slade's got thousands of dollars tied up in those flocks, not to mention his need to get them into the mountains. If we can pull it off it might be just what we need to throw that bunch from hell to breakfast."

"But how *could* we, Mike—just the three of us? You said yourself Smith would be suspicious—"

"I'm countin' on it."

"And his crew! He's bound to have a tough outfit."

She looked at him anxiously. "Wouldn't it be better if we went to Jeff Douglas and told him—"

"All our lovely suspicions?" Stroud laughed shortly. "You're forgettin' he sent me here. Alone. For a purpose. It's our only chance, Cindy. We've got to stop them."

Cindy drew a deep breath. "And then?"

"I stop Wafer."

FROM their place of concealment among the crags they saw the first of the sheep moving into the valley just as the rising sun flung its beading of gold across the east ramparts. By eight o'clock the valley was filled with them but Smith was too cagey to bunch the sheep there. Before he let his men eat he had them drift the gray flocks well up on the eastern slope where he could easily watch both ends of the valley.

By nine o'clock the sheepmen's fires were sending up fragrant curls of blue smoke. Cindy stared at them wistfully and Stroud, gaunt himself, knew she must be ravenous. But there was nothing he could do about it. He dared not even knock over a rabbit lest the sound of the shot attract Smith's notice.

He tightened his belt. "Dodgin' the law is a hungry business."

Cindy flashed him a smile. "It will take more than hunger to get rid of me, Mike."

At ten Chuck Murgatroyd rejoined them. "Saltiest bunch I've moved in a long time—damn near lost 'em comin' off that mountain."

Stroud asked, "How many?"

"Shovin' close to fifty. How many in that saddle band?"

"Enough," Stroud said, "if we can get them to running."

Murgatroyd studied the eastern slope. "That Smith is no fool. Notice how he's got those sheep spread out? From where he's sittin' he can watch both ways. He won't be caught nappin'."

"Hope not," Stroud grunted.

Murgatroyd considered him. "Well, it's your show." He gave Cindy a grin. "Want to sharpen your choppers? Here's some stuff I dug out of the Boxed Circle line camp." He produced some chipped beef from the pockets of his shirt. "Won't help your thirst but it may keep the flaps of your stomach unstuck."

"Chuck," Cindy cried, "you're a wizard!"

She was dividing the dried meat into three little piles when Murgatroyd said, "That's for you an' the boss. I don't want no more."

"You eat it, Cindy," Stroud said. "I—"

"Either we'll all have a part of it or Chuck can put the darn stuff right back in his pocket."

As the long morning dragged by it became obvious Smith had no intention of moving the sheep short of dark. Some time after noon Murgatroyd said, "There's a spring down the draw just below that pen where I put the broncs. Why don't you an' Cindy, Mike, take our horses down there and get them a drink?"

"Good idea. We'll all get a drink. Not much sense hangin' round any longer. We could figure all night, but when it's all cut an' dried this whole damn deal depends on the timin'—on whether or not Smith'll swallow the bait. Let's go."

AROUND the middle of the afternoon Cheyenne

Smith, standing guard above the sheep, saw three distant riders quartering south along the rim of the valley's western slope. Stroud knew Smith saw them because he jumped to his feet and started waving his arms. Below his vision they cut around a hogback and came out again where he had first caught sight of them. There were two other men with Smith now and Stroud didn't think they were discussing the weather. Leaving Cindy to wait, he and Murgatroyd once more spurred their ponies around the narrow ridge. But the herders had quit watching. Smith had his whole crew busy moving sheep, hurrying them down off the mountainside into the concealment of the valley below.

"That what you wanted?" Murgatroyd asked, and Stroud nodded.

"Those sheep'll be blattin' their heads off now. You fetch the broncs. Cindy an' me will take care of the saddle stock."

When they appeared an hour later on the western slope near the valley's south end, chasing back and forth to round up their remuda and weld it into a movable unit, Stroud told Cindy it was pretty obvious what Smith was up to. Many years in the business of caring for woollies had taught McClannigan's boss herder into what small bounds his flocks could be packed. When Cindy looked there wasn't a sheep in sight. Stroud said it was dollars to doughnuts Smith had bedded them down in the gorge of Long Pass where he could hold them bunched with two or three men while he deployed the rest of his rifle-packing bravos for battle. Whether he imagined he'd seen Randymier or not, he was in hostile country and would know any riders he saw to be cowmen. "Figurin' to take no chances," Stroud told Cindy, "he's put those sheep right where I want 'em."

They soon had the tame saddle band bunched just inside the valley's south opening. "I'll take the east side an' you take the west. Just keep them settled till you hear the wild bunch comin' through that crotch, then get out of the way."

They hadn't long to wait.

With a ground-shaking rumble of pounding hoofs Murgatroyd's broncs boiled through the south slot like hell wouldn't have them. They slowed a little tearing past the remuda, but only for an instant. With Murgatroyd behind and Stroud and Cindy on either flank yelling and waving and firing their six-shooters the whole bunch lit out for Long Pass like an avalanche; and ten minutes later there weren't enough sheep left to put in your eye.

24

STIRRUP SERENADE

IT was two hours past dark with no moon showing when Stroud stopped his horse a hundred yards from Stirrup's buildings. Cindy and Murgatroyd pulled up beside him. There was nothing to hear but the trembling leaves, nothing to see but a foreshortened horizon of disjointed shadows.

"Too damn black an' quiet," whispered Murgatroyd. "Can't tell where you're at or who's watchin' you."

"I don't think anyone's watchin'," Stroud murmured. "I think they're all out scourin' the hills."

"I'd feel a heap better if we could see a light."

"We're back of the barn," Cindy said. "We can't see the house. It's about two hundred feet dead ahead of us."

"We'll leave the horses," Stroud decided, and they all swung down. "We'll put them in the barn. Then, if they nicker, no one'll think much about it. Don't try to be too cautious now, just act like we belong here."

Murgatroyd said, "I don't like it," but he followed the others around to the barn's entrance.

"I'll wait out here," Stroud said, "in case anyone comes up. Put the horses in stalls but leave the gear on them."

"They're goin' to be hard to get at if we happen to need 'em."

"We won't have them to use if they happen to be discovered," Stroud answered; and Murgatroyd shrugged, took the reins of Stroud's horse and followed Cindy inside.

Stroud lounged by the door with his eyes open, thinking. Wafer might not be home. As Murgatroyd had said, it was awfully quiet. But it would be, of course, if the crew were out hunting them. Perhaps they were with Redcliff, a part of the sheriff's posse.

He said as the others rejoined him, "Sure the house is over that way? I don't see any lights."

"We wouldn't, from here," Cindy answered. "The main room's in the front and it faces the gate. We came in the back way. There—now you can see it."

All Stroud could see was a more substantial bit of gloom but as they crossed the yard the house took shape, a low rambling structure. He caught the soft whir of a windmill's blades.

"There's a veranda across the front," Cindy whispered. "You'll see it directly. Be careful going onto it, the third step creaks. There . . . see the lights? Both those windows open into the same room."

Stroud could hear the sound of voices; he heard Dan Wafer's distinctly, though not what he said. Reaching the steps he put out a hand, checking Cindy and Murgatroyd. Though the shades were drawn, thus preventing them from seeing who was in the room with Wafer, both the windows were open. "Just a minute," he breathed. "We better make sure how many's in there with him. Sounds like an argument."

"I don't care about that," a man's voice said, coldly angry. "When I gave you that money it was on the strict understanding I was to get your help—"

"You've had my help an' still have it," Wafer grumbled. "My help an' better than half my profits. What the hell are you beefin' about? I've kept my part of the bargain. You got your sheep through the—"

"We're not discussing my sheep. We're talking about Three Sixes. I haven't seen any signs of being cut in on that."

"Uncle Tal," Cindy whispered.

Stroud nodded. "Slade McClannigan."

"—about that when you gave me the stake. It's what I wanted it for, so's I could be in a position to bust the damn outfit. I told you all that. Her father—"

"All I want is my share of the profits."

"Profits!" Wafer shouted. "Where's there any profit in a gutted ranch?"

"That's what I've been asking myself. It may interest you to know—if you don't know already—that I've been staying at Three Sixes, making out to be the old man's brother, a bleary-eyed boozer I chanced to meet in California. Recalling your strange obsession, I thought it might pay me to cultivate his acquaintance. The man's memory was remarkable. He was here, you know, when they dug—"

"Suppose you get down to cases."

"I'm no fool, Dan. No man in his right mind would think of carrying a grudge so far as deliberately to ruin a valuable piece of property and then, having ruined it, spend three times what it would bring on the market buying up a piece of paper—''

McClannigan's voice broke off in the crash of a kicked back chair. A girl's scream climbed above the tumult and was lost in the racketing bang of a pistol.

Stroud would have dived at once for the doorway had not Murgatroyd's hand, with surprising strength, reached out and rooted him. *"Wait!"*

There followed a moment of intense stillness during which they heard nothing but the slap of a blind and the waterfall murmur of wind in the branches.

The girl's voice came then—Beulah May's, harsh and high strung with shock. "Where in Christ's name was the sense in that, Slade?"

"You saw his eyes! You saw him jump from his chair—"

"But the fool didn't even have hold of his—"

"I've had enough of his damn double dealing! He knew well as I do there's oil on that place. You think I'm going to sit twiddling my thumbs while a skunk like that does me out of a fortune? Get hold of yourself and help me find that note."

"But his crew—"

"They're off helping Redcliff. Don't stand there, dammit! Take a look in that desk while I go through his pockets."

"I don't like it, Slade. You're getting too careless. Who are you intending to pin this one on?"

There was a quick stamp of feet, the sound of flesh striking flesh. McClannigan's voice, tight with fury, snarled: "Now do what you're told and keep your jaw shut!"

STROUD shook Murgatroyd's hand off his shoulder. "I'll go in by the door—you cover me from the window . . ." He paused for an instant, head turned sideways, thinking to have caught some sound behind them. But his stare found nothing in that black mass of shadows and he faced front again. "Move the same time I do and maybe you can get there without being heard. Ready?"

"Ready."

Stroud was up the steps in one bound. Two floor-shaking strides took him across the veranda. He kicked down the door and went in through the smoke of McClannigan's pistol. But his eyes were trying to see too much at once. He stumbled over the body of Wafer, tripping headlong just as the sheep king fired. He'd backed into a corner and fired again before Stroud could bring his gun into action. It was no one's fault but Stroud's own for he'd been trying to watch out for Beulah May, too. The slug cut past within an inch of his ear and before McClannigan could rip loose another Stroud kicked the pistol out of his hand.

Not till then did he realize the shade was off one window. That was when he saw Murgatroyd, cursing and groaning, sprawled across the ledge with the shade crumpled under him, trying to get the hung gun from his offside holster.

Even as Stroud looked a slug spattered glass from a picture behind him and he flung himself sideways, driving two shots through the open window at the place where he'd seen the muzzle flash. He fired once more, heard a lifting yell and saw the man reel into the light from the window. It was Cheyenne Smith and he went down on his face.

"No you don't!" Cindy cried, and Stroud's jerked-around glance found her prodding McClannigan back into the room.

"This is all a mistake," the sheep king was muttering, but he shut his mouth when he saw Stroud's eyes.

"I'll take care of him now," Stroud said. "Take a look at Chuck, Cindy, an' see if you can tie up that hole in his—"

Murgatroyd said, "It ought to be in my head and then maybe somebody could see what's ailin' me. Standin' plumb in front of a lighted window!"

He sighed, shook his head and got onto his feet waving Cindy away. He considered the dead man, then walked over to McClannigan.

"Start talkin'."

"I'll talk, all right, when I see my attorney!"

Beulah May, looking up from powdering her nose, said, "Who are we going to pin this one on, honey? You damn sure aren't going to hang it on me and you've already fixed Stroud up with Angus. Kind of looks like you're stuck with it, doesn't it . . . *dearie?*"

Murgatroyd gave her an interested look. "Are you intending to suggest that Slade killed his brother?"

Beulah May smiled. "Didn't you know that?"

"You lying slut!" screamed McClannigan.

"Shut up," Stroud said, and slammed him into a chair.

Murgatroyd asked, "Can you prove that, ma'am?"

"Well, I didn't actually see him shove the knife in, but I think I can make out a pretty good case . . . if it should be worth my while."

Murgatroyd twisted his head around to Cindy. "I expect you can start gettin' your stuff together."

"Stuff?"

Murgatroyd said with a mischievous grin, "Goin' to marry the guy, ain't you? Wouldn't surprise me at all to find they've turned him loose once Jeff gets that report I'm goin' to write."

Stroud stared. *"You're* goin' to write?"

Murgatroyd laughed. "Hadn't you guessed? I'm Jeff's chief trouble shooter."

Raw, fast-action adventure from one of the world's favorite Western authors

MAX BRAND

writing as Evan Evans

0-515-08898-6	**SILVERTIP'S STRIKE**	$2.75
0-515-08909-5	**THE WHITE CHEYENNE**	$2.75
0-515-08939-7	**THE SEVENTH MAN**	$2.75
0-515-08897-5	**TWENTY NOTCHES**	$2.75
0-515-08962-1	**FIRE BRAIN**	$2.75

0-515-08582-0	**STRANGE COURAGE**	$2.75
0-515-08611-8	**MONTANA RIDES AGAIN**	$2.75
0-515-08692-4	**THE BORDER BANDIT**	$2.75
0-515-08711-4	**SIXGUN LEGACY**	$2.50
0-515-08776-9	**SMUGGLER'S TRAIL**	$2.50
0-515-08759-9	**OUTLAW VALLEY**	$2.95
0-515-08885-4	**THE SONG OF THE WHIP**	$2.75

WANTED:
Hard Drivin' Westerns From
J.T.Edson

J.T. Edson's famous "Floating Outfit" adventure books are on every Western fan's **MOST WANTED** list. Don't miss _any_ of them!

___	THE COLT AND THE SABRE	09341-7/$2.50
___	GO BACK TO HELL	09101-5/$2.50
___	HELL IN THE PALO DURO	09361-1/$2.50
___	THE HIDE AND TALLOW MEN	08744-1/$2.50
___	THE QUEST FOR BOWIE'S BLADE	09113-9/$2.50
___	RETURN TO BACKSIGHT	09397-2/$2.50
___	SET TEXAS BACK ON HER FEET	08651-8/$2.50
___	THE TEXAS ASSASSIN	09348-4/$2.50
___	THE TRIGGER MASTER	09087-6/$2.50
___	THE REBEL SPY	09646-7/$2.50
___	APACHE RAMPAGE	09714-5/$2.50
___	TERROR VALLEY	09569-X/$2.50
___	WACO'S DEBT	08528-7/$2.50

*Blazing heroic adventures
of the gunfighters of the WILD WEST
by Spur Award-winning author*

LEWIS B. PATTEN

____ **THE RUTHLESS RANGE**   0-441-74181-9/$2.50

____ **THE STAR AND THE GUN**   0-441-77955-7/$2.50

____ **CHEYENNE DRUMS**   0-441-10370-7/$2.50

____ **THE RED SABBATH**   0-441-71173-1/$2.50

____ **GIANT ON HORSEBACK**   0-441-28816-2/$2.50